The Chronicles of All-Time

Dear Joey Silva

Life is a journey.

Go slow, go fast,

Savor, relax, feel, blend.

The name of the game: Even when you think you're doing it wrong, you're doing it right!

Trust me.

01/17/2015

The Chronicles of All-Time

Remember to Forget

Written and illustrated by

Dr. Jurgen Vanhauwe

Library of Congress Control Number: 2014920735
ISBN: Hardcover 978-1-5035-1852-0
Softcover 978-1-5035-1853-7
eBook 978-1-5035-1854-4

This is a work of fiction. Names, characters, places and incidents either are the product of the author's imagination or are used fictitiously, and any resemblance to any actual persons, living or dead, events, or locales is entirely coincidental.

Author photograph by:
Andrey Tokarev, centaurphotolab.com

This book was printed in the United States of America.

Rev. date: 11/21/2014

To order additional copies of this book, contact:
Xlibris
1-888-795-4274
www.Xlibris.com
Orders@Xlibris.com
656924

CONTENTS

Also by Dr. Jurgen Vanhauwe

Waking up at both sides

Dedicated to My Greatest Teacher:

with love, for love.

SUCCEEDING TO FAIL

HARMONIC UNIVERSE ONE. Twenty-First Century. Planet Earth.

The command center of the starship *Hawk* circling Earth is lit up like a Christmas tree.

"Alert! Alert! Integrity breach in Hangars 1 and 4."

Alfie's slender body moves quickly among the main consoles, taking inventory of the ship's systems; he reports to the captain.

"Captain, we cannot stay much longer. We are sustaining too much damage. We are securing our agents and as many selected indigenous humans as we can. They are being beamed to the decks. All hangars are being cleared, and all aircraft carriers are safely inside."

"Did we get Commander Jane Darkon on board?"

"Yes. Barely. She is in quarantine for removal of spyware and tracers. That is how our Geeray foes could target us. They used her like a Trojan horse. We cannot hold up the frequency barriers to protect ourselves, let alone the Earth."

"This is not how I imagined this would go, Alfie. The council will not be happy, and neither will Jane."

A shudder throws two crewmen on the ground, more lights lit up.

"Captain, our T'Rill main power cores have been hit by annihilation beams. The Geeray must have access to our frequencies and defense pattern rotators. The ship is beyond repairs and is falling apart quickly."

"Evacuate all personnel and send out a call for help now!"

Explosions are not heard in space, but the destruction of the *Hawk* starship was seen in the night sky from the Persian Gulf till Iceland.

On the *Falcon* starship positioned behind Saturn.

"Captain Kyrasha, we have an emergency distress call from the Hawk."

"Open a channel and ask how we can help. What is their location?"

"Unable to open a communication channel. Their last location was around Earth. I can only pick up debris. The Hawk is gone."

"That is impossible. The Geeray are technologically unable to locate our trans-dimensional ships or penetrate our shields."

"Looks like they found a way how to do it, Captain."

"Any escape pod survivors?"

"A few, yes. One is in a quarantine cylinder. I recommend we beam them aboard from our current location. The Earth grid is dangerously unstable."

"Get a lock on all survivors and get them to the medical bay as soon as possible."

Thirteen hours later, Commander Jane Darkon awakens from the quarantine cylinder.

"What happened, Jane?" Kyrasha asks with a frown, his face full of concern.

"One moment I am in California, and the next moment I am in a quarantine cylinder. A bit later I am ejected into space, and I see a starship explode. Now I am here. That is it in a nutshell. Where am I?"

"On board the starship *Falcon*, Intergalactic Federation starship. You are safe here. I am Captain Kyrasha."

"I felt them all die, Captain Kyrasha, when the Hawk exploded. It is all my fault."

"Relax, Commander Darkon. You went through a lot. We will be home soon. We will reach the star gates system in forty-four minutes. And Alcyone is our home base too, so we can celebrate when we get there."

"So the mission succeeded?"

"Everything is a success, Jane, even so-called failure. Didn't you teach us that?"

"Right. Did we save humanity and planet Earth?"

"We have successfully evacuated thirty-three million humans. A majority of our reincarnated agents have been recovered and are in memory retrieval units, so they can take up their normal lives."

"Thirty-three million people on this ship? What about Earth?"

"The Earth grid became unstable, and Earth imploded in this reality. There are many realities left where Earth still exists. The thirty-three million humans have been collected by extracting their consciousness and DNA. They are stored in our palladium silver crystals, and they are living in a holographic projection. To them, they are still on Earth living a normal life. They are safe, but we will need to reeducate them. Their bodies will be rebuilt once a Federation planet agrees to adopt them. This time we hope the integration goes smoothly."

"This time?"

"We have been doing this over and over, Jane. Leading them safely out of Egypt, then out of Germany and Poland to a patch of land they called Israel, their holy land. Do you see the similarities here? What happens on a small scale happens on a larger scale. Now, instead of finding a new piece of land, we are trying to find them a new planet. The problem just gets bigger when it remains unresolved.

"Time does not exist, remember? We are reliving our dramas until we learn. If we can introduce humans peacefully to their next 'holy land,' then retroactively peace will come to previous timelines, or future ones. Now, if the humans would have realized this from their own historical records, they probably would have acted differently in Egypt, Israel, and other war zones. We are all One. How hard is this concept to get? It is so easy, yet some timelines keep fighting because of racial, gender, religious, or political differences. And eventually that comes to us, so we have to go back in time, and reeducate ourselves. Funny, isn't it?"

"It would be if not for all those lives lost and all the pain and horror. I am not fully aware yet. Did the memory retrieval unit malfunction?"

"I actually wanted to talk to you about that. You suffered severe withdrawal symptoms when we allowed you to experience all that you are. The polarity consciousness and the traumas you have experienced on Earth are the source of the problem—level three post-traumatic stress disorder. You cannot return to your previous self without the resolution of these events, or you would cause damage to yourself and many others."

"Can't we just delete the traumas from my memory?"

"Ah yes, we have tried that already in an alternate Universe. We learned that the deletion of these energies from your system, a purging as we call it, allows for the energies to float around in subspace until they find a suitable partner, and then they amplify the original signature in another Universe. It is like one droplet of oil finding another droplet of oil in water. When these droplets combine, the resulting droplet is larger. You may get a chuckle out of knowing that the bigger problem manifested in the other Universe to the ones who caused you your traumas, so your so-called nemeses could feel the amplified effect firsthand. Now, in this Universe we sense that amplified effect on a deeper level. We all feel it, but since we can tap into universal love quite easily, the effect on our neurological systems is cushioned."

"So, now what, Captain Kyrasha?" Jane asks.

"Well, while we were being space cowboys, our researchers in Wakala, an off-world planet, have created a new treatment, and we are hoping you would want to try it out."

"Can I ask what it is all about?"

Captain Kyrasha smiles. "First, let me get the designer of the experimental treatment on line. He is a synthetic engineer expert, Dr. Alfred Brobol."

A few flicks on the projected monitors with her slender fingers, and a friendly middle-aged face appears on the projected screen.

ARTIFICIAL RECOVERY CYBORG

HARMONIC UNIVERSE FOUR. 3.8 Million Years AD, Planet Wakala.

"Captain Kyrasha, Alfred Brobol here. An honor to meet one of our fleet captains. How can I help you?"

"Dr. Brobol, one of our commanders is suffering from level three post-traumatic stress disorder due to exposure to third dimensional polarity events propagated by the Geeray. We would like to know more about your technology to treat the underlying energies."

"Oh well, of course." A broad smile appears across his silver-haired head, and his emerald green eyes beam with a hint of pride. "Well, we have created a three-dimensional surrogate matrix, very similar to your palladium silver crystals. This matrix can hold her consciousness, which will be downloaded into an Artificial Recovery Cyborg in that matrix. Basically, the DNA of the clone will be optimized to her energies to counterbalance the energies of her underlying traumas, and Commander Darkon will relive some of the traumas at lower and lower intensities until they reach baseline levels. When that occurs, her consciousness will be uploaded from the cyborg and downloaded in her current body, which we will keep in bio-stasis."

"How long does the treatment last?"

"In the virtual reality, it can be months, years, decades, or lifetimes, but in our time, it is a matter of days to a few months maximum."

"A few months? What about my family?"

"They can visit you any time they want. In fact, we encourage it. They can download in the program for a short visit, like a chance encounter. Longer visits can be arranged for family members or close friends, who can help serve as mentors in the recovery process. But you will not recognize them as such."

"Why not?"

"Your memory is failing you. Humanity was created as a hybrid species by what humans call gods. It is only a genetic experiment, just like planet Earth. Over millions of years, we humans have evolved beyond what you can imagine. The human race evolved according to their multi-stranded DNA into many hybrid species, some more feline, some more canine or dolphin-like, etc. That DNA was donated by a variety of star families, each bringing unique gifts to every individual. You may have observed this from the time/space coordinate where you came from. There were some people who displayed enlarged canine teeth. Their dormant canine DNA was waking up. You were in the middle of the Grand Awakening until that timeline was cut short. Our Creators orchestrated this multi-hybrid approach to ensure the largest diversity possible, because that is how the survival rate of large ecosystems is maximized. Strength through diversity. If you always learn in the same way, with the same senses, with the same mind-set, with the same DNA, then very little progress can be made. We are united through our differences and our similarities. The generations of humans that you experienced on earth, Jane, are from the third and fourth seeding in an evolutionary timeline of about one hundred thousand years. Imagine what is possible when you would evolve for almost four million years, which is where I am relative to you."

"But you look similar to me. And so does Captain Kyrasha and the entire medical staff."

"Holographic image inducers, let us call it highly evolved, make up from your perspective. We appear different to you than what we are in a way that is appealing to you. I assure you, we look quite different. And that is why you would not recognize your friends or family. This is a precaution we have taken to make you feel as comfortable as possible during the treatment."

"Would you mind turning off your image inducers for me?"

"Are you sure you are mentally ready to experience that?"

"I think so, Dr. Brobol. Yes."

Dr. Brobol taps behind his ears; his face becomes fuzzy and pixelated and then reappears as a blue elongated face with widened smurfish eyes and a dolphin-like mouth. The emerald-green eyes look so much bigger and even more endearing. A nervous smile follows.

"Oh, wow!" gasps Jane Darkon.

A CALL FOR HELP

HARMONIC UNIVERSE ONE. Twenty-First Century. Planet Earth.

Dr. Elliott Himmerept, born in Belgium in 1973, is reminiscing about his wonderful childhood with two amazing parents who raised him very diligently and in a very effective manner, or at least he thinks so.

Rashelle is sitting behind her antique wooden desk and is trying to understand his situation. "So, there was very little childhood trauma, and you were very well supported and loved by your parents. They never divorced and you lived in the same house during your childhood and teenage years. Looks like a very stable environment to me. What happened in your late adolescent years?"

"Well, at the age of eighteen, I went to college to study chemistry and biochemistry. I had a great time in college with many new friends. It was not always easy, and it required a lot of hard work to finally graduate magna cum laude. After that, I decided to continue my studies and obtain a doctorate degree in biochemistry."

"All right, Dr. Himmerept, so you are very smart, book smart. How about life experience?"

"Well, when I left home, my mom said, 'Elliott, be careful, it is a very dangerous world out there. Do not trust anyone.' That was about the only advice about living life that I received from her. Needless to say I am not the most street-smart person on the planet. In fact, I think it is one of my endearing qualities: I was—and I still am—a very gullible person. I believe in the good of people. But science trained me to keep a skeptical mind and to always question the validity of conclusions without seeing the facts or data. Book smarts and a skeptical analysis method are an important piece of training that I received during my education."

"That all sounds good. What happened after you graduated?"

"I went to study at the Northwestern University of Chicago to continue my studies in neuroscience, mainly about signaling pathways in the brain and in blood vessels. I have always been fascinated with studying receptors in the brain that affect neurological or neurochemical pathways involved in paranoia or delusion. I am so fascinated by how the brain works, because to me, it truly is the most complicated organ of the human body."

"What did you do when you completed your postdoctoral fellowship?"

"I entered into the private business area, and I landed jobs for technical sales in various firms where I was successful to the extent that I ended up in challenging managerial positions. It was very rewarding work, and I learned many things, but I decided eventually to turn back to technical sales because I needed a little break from managing people and global portfolios. And I was beginning to experience that the fast-paced entertainment life and the fast-paced business life are not always compatible. 'Work hard and party hard' used to be my motto, but I am being forced to reevaluate that statement."

"So basically, you were living life on the high road, and you needed to take a few steps back because of your health issues that are now coming up."

"Yes. Exactly. Could it be that these health issues are related to the stress of purchasing a new home, my partner moving to Brazil, and my friend's suicide attempt?"

"Yes. That could be. Before we go there, can you tell me a bit more about your health issues?"

"Well, I was recently diagnosed with sleep apnea, and now my thoughts are too fast and I have trouble concentrating. I am sleeping with a CPAP machine, and I seem to need sleeping pills to keep my mind quiet so I can fall asleep. So I decided it was time to take action, but before going the commercial medicine route, I was thinking that maybe I needed to try something holistic first. I'm not sure why, but there is no harm in trying it out, right?"

Rashelle starts explaining how the treatment will be performed and what might possibly happen during and after the treatment. Meantime,

Elliott is looking at this lady quite amused, yet in need of help, so he is trying to understand this strong-willed woman, a holistic healer that came highly recommended by one of his colleagues.

"I think I can treat your racing thoughts. Of course, there are no guarantees for success, but if you are open to the idea I just presented, we can move ahead right now."

"Let me get this straight. I'm going to lie back, relax, and close my eyes. In the meantime, you will be calling in energies and so-called higher entities to treat these symptoms, which you believe are the manifestation of unbalanced energies somewhere within or around me in my past, present, or future timeline. Is that the gist of it?"

"That is a good way of looking at it. Yes. It is much more complex than that, but I like the way you summarized our conversation."

"Do you know how crazy that sounds? I am a scientist. My customers are researchers trying to find cures, and I mean real medicines for cancer, Alzheimer, allergies, infections, and so on. For crying out loud, I studied dopamine and serotonin signaling pathways involved in brain circuitry. You are asking me to leave behind twenty-two years of scientific education and experience and just take your word for it?"

"Dr. Himmerept, I'm asking you to be open to the idea that there might be alternative ways to treat your symptoms, not abandon your previous belief systems. Why else did you come here? You could have asked for a Ritalin prescription, and yet you are sitting here in front of me."

"All right, but I have to admit I am slightly uncomfortable with the idea. But if there is a possibility that you, or whoever else, can make these racing thoughts go away, then I say I am all for it."

"Great! Now, please lie back in that chair behind you. Make yourself comfortable, close your eyes, take five deep relaxing breaths, and I will be right with you."

Elliott complies while his mind is still racing at 260 miles an hour, and suddenly he feels like he is being probed with sonar or something similar that is very gentle in nature. His abdomen heats up tremendously, and he thinks she put some infrared light on that region to stimulate blood flow. The probing is not random but very delicate and directed to different body parts, almost in an intelligent manner. Memories of early childhood and teenage years flash by: playing in the garden at grandma's place, windsurfing at Lake Como in Italy, skiing in Davos in Switzerland with his parents, etc.

Elliott wonders, *"What a nice trip into the past, but I'm still thinking way too fast despite the comfortable relaxation I'm experiencing,"* and soon after he "feels" a tweezers-like device aspirating at his left temple while energy is leaving through the skull and suddenly . . . peace of mind. Finally.

Elliott's mental faculties say, *"How did she manage to do that? I've been meditating or trying to quiet my mind for the past three days without much success, and she gets it done in less than fifteen minutes. Mental note: I need to understand more about the process she is using. This is phenomenal!"*

And the process continues until energy is now flowing inwards at various points of entry throughout his slim, toned body. When the energy is pushed in his left and right lower arms, the energy infusion accelerates and exceeds Elliott's pain threshold rather abruptly. He jerks upward, opens his eyes, and there is Rashelle, still sitting behind her desk with eyes closed and hands waving ominously in the air.

Elliott wonders, *"Huh? Wasn't she standing next to me using infrared lights or magnets, or warm stones and the like? I definitely need to learn more about this."*

Rashelle (eyes closed) says, "Lie back, relax, we are not done yet. The energy flow will be gentler this time so you can handle it."

THE PIGEON HAS LANDED

HARMONIC UNIVERSE ONE. Twenty-First Century. Planet Earth.

"Elliott, you really need to start believing in a deity. Jesus, Buddha, Shiva, Allah. Anyone. Whoever you choose."

"Why, Rashelle? As I mentioned, I'm a scientist, and I abandoned the Catholic Church a long time ago. So far, I have seen no evidence that 'God' exists, so if it can't be proven to exist in a controlled environment in a repetitive and reproducible manner, then it stands to reason that 'it' doesn't exist."

Rashelle's exasperated sigh speaks volumes. "Do you accept that you experienced something that is out of this world during your previous healing session?"

"I admit that I can't explain why and how I felt those bodily sensations, and I was impressed that you were able to get rid of my racing thoughts in only one session. That's why I'm here. I want to learn the type of methodology you are using so I can understand it from the inside out. But I wouldn't go that far to say that it had anything to do with Jesus or Buddha or whoever. It just needs to be further investigated, and I'm glad that you accepted to teach me how you go about your healing ways. Energy healing, as you call it."

"Elliot, you are going to work with energy and forces beyond your control and comprehension. For your own safety and sanity, please make an effort to connect this week with any deity or at least entertain the possibility that there might be something more. Can you promise me that?"

"Fine, if it makes you feel better. How do I do that?"

"Just close your eyes and ask for guidance from a higher power."

"It doesn't make sense, but I can promise to try. I can't promise it will work though."

Later that night, before going to bed, Elliott is a bit apprehensive, but decides to give it a try anyway.

"At least no one can make fun of me as I'm doing this all alone in my bedroom, and I'm guessing there is nothing to lose but fifteen minutes of my time."

Elliot closes his eyes and asks for guidance from a higher power. Nothing happens at first, and in that time, his elaborate scientific mind comes on board and starts looking at the back of his eyelids. Overanalyzing is one of Elliott's strengths and weaknesses.

"I see red because the blood vessels contain red blood cells that carry hemoglobin, which turns blood red. Hence, I see mostly red. Hmmm, eyelids are turning yellowish. This should not be happening. Why is that? Blue, I could understand if I were oxygen deprived, but I'm not. Am I?"

And the yellow turns into a bright white cloud with—on top—what appears to be the image of a white bird flapping its wings. The tail cannot be seen because the latter part of the body is consumed by the white energy cloud.

"Looks like a pigeon to me," thinks Elliott. *"Great, I'm seeing a pigeon. That's stupid."* So he opens his eyes and gives himself a pat on the back for having an overactive imagination and goes to bed.

The next day, he tells last night's meditation story to Jeff, one of his friends who works in an upscale clothing store as a manager. Jeff replies, "You mean you saw a dove?"

"Jeff, English is my second language. Remember, I'm from Belgium. What is a dove?"

Jeff laughs, "It's a white pigeon. You know some people might believe that you just saw the Holy Spirit."

"OK, Jeff, that is a bit far-fetched. Don't you think? If so, the Holy Spirit didn't say much at all. Maybe it's a mute Holy Spirit?" Elliott sends one of his agreeable smiles with his pearly white teeth, and continues, "You know what's going to be hard, Jeff? No caffeine, no alcohol, no meat and preferably raw vegetables until my next session with energy lady Rashelle. That's what she asked me to abide by in preparation for our next session. I started this morning, and I'm a bit on edge. But I'm determined to see this through. No pain no gain. I can do this."

"Good luck with that, Elliott. I'm guessing you're going to call me when you need a friend to talk you through meat or Hefeweizen cravings?"

"I won't be calling you, Jeff. You would only tempt me and enjoy my situation. I'd probably call on Beckster instead. He's a bit more empathic than you are."

"Beckster? I'll have a chat with him and see what I can do to get him on my side. Is he still working as a technician?" Jeff laughs.

"Don't start, Jeff. You know he is sensitive about that."

THE NIGHT OF THE ARENA

HARMONIC UNIVERSE ONE. Twenty-First Century. Planet Earth.

Elliott shuts down his laptop. All sales quotes, technical reports, and data sheets are sent out to his customers; he can go to bed knowing that all is taken care off. He loves his customers—typically scientific researchers in the biotechnology or biomedical field. The discussions they throw around about possible ways to tackle a given research topic or technical issue often stimulate his mind, and Elliott loves using his analytical mind, an asset he is righteously proud of. That night, however, his marvelous mind would meet its first Waterloo, and not like in a happy-go-lucky Abba song. Twenty minutes after turning off his bedside lamp, an energy beam envelops his entire head. His eyelids start fluttering at an uncomfortable speed, and thousands of images are streaming in. There are too many images coming in to consciously process any one. Obviously, getting sleep is the last thing on his mind.

"What is going on? Am I consciously awake during REM sleep? No! That can't be it. In REM, the pupil moves quickly. These are my eyelids, and the frequency is much higher than REM. All right, relax, why am I seeing images and symbols and diagrams? Can I pick any of them out? No, I can barely think myself. The source seems to be coming from the other side of the beam. This is borderline painful, I am not going to sleep while this is going on. Let's wait and see what happens next."

His scientific mind frantically continues to try and analyze what is going on.

"I'm having my own Jill Bolte Taylor moment. However, this doesn't feel like a stroke."

Having studied the biochemistry of the brain, this event presents a fascinating challenge, and while intriguing at first, the process continues for too long and Elliott's brain is not making any headway trying to diagnose the source of this symptom. The best he can come up with is those darn green vegetables. So when reason fails, panic sets in. Many unkosher words fill the now-lit-up room. Finally he decides to get up and start looking for a sleeping pill, and solace comes from a voice out of nowhere. "Relax. This process will take a few hours. Please don't take the sleeping pill. You will be fully energized in the morning." And indeed, it takes about two hours until the fluttering of eyelids and the stream of images stop. Peace at last, but not for long.

Next, Elliott becomes aware that he is in an arena, but he is also consciously aware that his physical body lies in bed with its eyes closed unable to move. The arena has three levels: the first level is circular with sand as the flooring material, white walls, and not any single visible exit. The second level is circular too, but it has balconies overlooking the arena. The walls are all white without any decorations, and Elliott spots about twenty humanoid entities; some have blue skin color and white hair—the so-called avatar-level. A circular opening in the ceiling looks out to a vast dark space of nothingness with only three beings sitting quietly and peering inside through the circular window. Elliott recognizes one as Buddha; then he notices a blue male figure with four arms, later to be identified as the Hindu God, Shiva, and the third being's identity remains elusive to say the least.

"My parents picked the wrong religion after all. Where is Jesus in all this? Grocery shopping?"

Surprisingly, Elliott feels at peace and eerily at home. "*It feels like I have been here before?*"

White bearded avatar: "*Yes, you have. Many times. Welcome back, Master Elliott. Let's see if you remember what you have already learned.*"

A metal-looking symbol, it feels like quicksilver, appears out of thin air and hovers in front of Elliott. It's about the same size as him and has the shape of an inward spiral ending in a vertical line that runs downward through the spiral.

"*Show us how to use this symbol in more than two dimensions.*"

Somehow, it is perfectly clear to Elliott to take the tip of the spiral at the center of the symbol and pull the quicksilver alive-feeling material toward himself to create a three dimensional spiral.

"That's great. Now use it in four dimensions. Then in five dimensions, and we also want to see how you would go to infinite dimensions."

With amazing ease, the solutions come to Elliott's mind, and he shows his audience how this can be achieved in more than one manner.

"Very good. What is the frequency of this symbol?"

"It depends on the perspective of the originator and its target, Avatar. It starts with the following tones and frequencies, and if originator and receiver are in tune, it will increase in frequency and amplitude to achieve the desired result."

Elliott creates the tones and frequencies in his mind, and all around seem to be able to receive them.

Elliott's mind gets sidetracked. *"How do I know this and how come these beings seem to be nodding approvingly? I'm not even talking with my mouth?"*

"Keep your focus, Master! A large part of you is well aware that you are not on the physical three-dimensional plane. At least, not with your consciousness. You will soon remember that your so-called physical reality is but a dream from the view point of this reality, and what happens here is more real than what you and your fellow human beings think is real. It's time to start shedding your indoctrination and pick up where you left off. Thought is a strong creative force in the Universe, and desire is one of the driving engines behind the expansion of our Universe. That said, it would be wise to not become attached to the expectations surrounding your desires, a feat that most humans seem to have difficulties with. We can hear your thoughts, and, as such, what you are experiencing is, from your viewpoint, telepathy, although that is a very narrow way of looking at it."

And so, the interactive lessons continue for hours until Elliott becomes aware that his body is in need of a bathroom break.

"Hey guys, I really need to pee here. And I don't want to pee in my bed."

"Very well. Your consciousness will return to your body, and when you are done, just lie down and you will return to this arena."

When Elliott lies down in the bed after his potty break, his consciousness is instantly transferred to the arena, and the lessons of remembrance continue till five o'clock in the morning, at which point he falls asleep instantly. The next day, Elliott is fully energized, but also a bit distraught, so he calls Rashelle.

"Rashelle, something strange happened last night. I think I might be going crazy. Can you tell me what is going on?"

"They are preparing you for our meeting on Saturday. Relax. Everything is going fine. Nothing to worry about. This is completely normal."

"Really? This is normal? In my field, this can be considered a psychotic breakdown. Maybe, it is a psychotic breakdown? I can't afford to have a meltdown. I have customers to take care of. My company is counting on me."

"And you can still do that. You will have a different point of view. That's all. In fact, you'll have a much broader perspective and, provided you integrate the knowledge harmoniously, you will be more successful than ever."

"If you say so. Are we still on for Saturday?"

"Yes, we are. I'm very much looking forward to it."

Later that night, Elliott calls his partner Josie, who is in Brazil for a long period of time. When he remembers that Josie was not comfortable with the idea of energy healing, he decides not to tell her about what happened in the arena, and they talk about their future plans. They have been together for six years in a long-distance relationship, and if they want to live together comfortably, they will have to get married so she can get a green card for the United States. Alternatively, Elliott could move to Brazil and find a job there. It remains an inconclusive conversation.

D-DAY

HARMONIC UNIVERSE ONE. Twenty-First Century. Planet Earth.

Elliott shows up at Rashelle's office full with anticipation after all the course work he went through that week. He's obviously eager to try out energy flowing through his cells and get more insight on the peculiar bodily sensations he felt during his previous healing session. Except, during this three-hour session he doesn't feel much and voices his concern.

"I'm not feeling much, Rashelle. Are you sure everything went fine?"

"Yes, I transferred the energies to you and opened up your channels. You should be able to sense something. OK, let's try this. Bring your two middle fingers closer to one another and see if you can feel a current running through or if you can see the current between your two fingers. Place your fingers at about half an inch from one another and make tiny circular movements with your fingertips."

"Oh yes, I can feel something. It's very mild though, almost imperceptible. I think I can see the current, though. Does it look like the shimmering air that we can see when looking right above the road at a hot day?"

"You got it! You can heal yourself now, or others. I suggest you start playing with how it feels within your body. Good luck, Elliott! Oh, and keep it slow the next few days and drink plenty of water, and still no alcohol."

Keeping it slow, to Elliott, means going out dancing at the local dance club Ricky's, but he refrains from drinking alcohol to strike a balance between guilt and pleasure. Strangely, he feels energy fields pushing against his own, then pulling him in, and this push-and-pull game is causing disorientation. To make matters worse, he observes green-and-red ghost images floating in front of the faces of some of his friends, but not all of them. And these floating images do not look inviting; they seem rather menacing and intimidating.

Elliott reaches out to Jeff, who is on the dance floor.

"Jeff, I'm not feeling well!" And as Jeff turns around, Elliott notices the floating red-and-green ghost images in front of Jeff's face.

"Are you all right? Are you drunk?"

"No, I'm not drunk. I've been nursing soda all night long."

In his mind Elliott is thinking, "*I can't tell Jeff how uncomfortable it is to talk to him while his ghost faces are staring me in the eyes. I got to go.*"

Jeff replies, "Wait a bit. Maybe it's the music. Or the people. Or you're just tired?"

"You know what. I'm going to leave. I probably should have stayed home anyway. It's been a busy week. Love you, Jeff."

"OK, call me in the morning and text me when you get home, just to make sure you're fine. Love you too."

While walking home, self-pity is kicking in. "*What have I done? How can I fix this? I can't tell anyone, or they will think I'm going crazy. Maybe I am going crazy? Ugh . . .*"

Elliott gets home and goes to sit down on the toilet bowl; while concentrating on relaxing muscles, he sees a bright spiral of energy coming down from the ceiling. It's about four inches wide but ends in a tip, and it's spiraling closer and closer to his head until the tip hits him right between the eyebrows. *Zap*!

One second later, Elliott is in "white energy land." There is white light all around him. He doesn't see with his eyes, but he sees the white energy with his consciousness; almost like how one sees when one is dreaming. He can't locate his physical body, but he is aware that he is somewhere while feeling infinite peace and ecstasy. And then he hears an older male's voice.

"*So, you're finally here. Ask me all your questions.*"

"*Where am I?*"

"*Well, in your concept of reality, and there are many realities, but what your consciousness can accept at this moment in time, you are in Heaven.*"

"Oh? OK. Oh, man, no one told me I should prepare a list of questions. Are you God?"

"I have many names."

"Are you the white pigeon I saw a few days ago?"

"Yes and no. But for what you mean, yes."

"Can I call you 'Pigeon'?"

"You can call me anything you want. And I'm quite fond of the name Pigeon. We are going to be laughing about that for a very long time."

"Is Jesus here?"

"Yes."

"Is Buddha here?"

"Yes."

Elliott pulls out a few other names including deceased relatives, other deities, and such. In short, everyone is having a party in white energy land. What a relief!

"Does Hell exist?"

"Not in the way that you think it exists. I never created Hell. Unconditional loves means without condition. It doesn't mean I love you when you do or don't do this, or if you believe this or that or not. It means no matter what you think or do, you are always loved. I love you so much that I allow you to think all the horrible things that you were taught, and as such you experience them. I'll tell you a little secret. The whole Universe is mental, meaning consciousness is the primary creative driver. So what you think and believe—or are fed to believe—can become your reality. So in that sense, you can create Hell where you live on Earth, or you can choose to create Heaven."

"Did I die?"

"No, you did not die."

"Then why am I here?"

"Because you agreed to forget, and I agreed to remind you. Right now, I am reminding you."

"Can I stay here?"

"No, you can't stay here."

"Why not?"

"Because you have work to do."

"What kind of work are we talking about?"

"You're going to tell people about this and many other experiences."

"I think you got the wrong guy. I don't know how I got here. I don't even believe in you."

"You are smart enough. You'll figure it out. You just need to remember. You, and many of your fellow human beings, have agreed to forget. And I have agreed to remind many, and you're an important tool in bringing back huge portions of memory to many beings. And when you're back in your body, I'll help you remember bit by bit."

"Strangely enough, that actually starts making sense. But why me?"

Rolling laughter ensues. *"Why not you? And, you're not the only one. There are many messengers like you, so don't stroke your ego, and I know you have a big one, Dr. Himmerept. My advice is to dissolve your ego and reassign its role in your reality experience. That's one of the keys to getting here, and there. As you were asking, you were raised a Catholic and believed in Me. You turned your back on your beliefs and your faith in Me in the process of becoming a scientist and integrating your father's belief system. You studied psychosis and paranoia. You're perfect for the job. Do you see the Divine irony here? That, and you were available. You volunteered for this."*

"I volunteered for this? Well, I'm not going to go stand on a corner with a sign that reads the-world-is-ending."

"I don't want you to. In fact, I want you to be as comfortable and at peace as you want to be. You volunteered for this before you became physical. I'm just here to get you back on the path of what you set out to do. Souls set up their lives before they go to Earth, with well-written and thought-out agreements between Myself and other Souls that reincarnate with them in the same space/time coordinates. These agreements can be changed at any given time in case you don't like your experience. You will remember more about these at a later time. Oh, and don't get yourself killed. I got plenty of those already."

The next moment, Elliott wakes up in the bathroom, still sitting down on the toilet bowl. Surprisingly, his body hasn't slumped to the floor, and he still needs to take care of bodily requirements. Elliott notes to himself that while he had an awareness of his body in the "Arena," there was no such thing while he was in white energy land.

THE LEMURIAN CANDIDATES

HARMONIC UNIVERSE TWO. 75,000 BC. Planet Earth. Kurt Couric and his best friend Cory Tantor are hastily walking through the long hallway adorned with octagon windows and diamond- or circular-shaped artwork that is framed with oak wood, laid in with precious stones like topaz and sapphires. The view outside is breathtaking: lush forests with green canopies contrasted by a crystal clear, deep blue sky and rivers feeding the ocean through an enormous patchwork of fields and crops. The Lemurians know very well how to integrate their advanced society into nature in a synergistic manner. But there are more pressing matters at hand.

At the end of the long hallway, two large cedarwood doors, engraved with two golden spirals, sway open to the council chamber. Kurt and Cory enter in their white togas. Their beards are neatly trimmed. An attitude of congeniality among all council members puts them at ease. The two of them stand in the middle of the luminescent arch-shaped table. At the apex of the table sits Chancellor David Troy. The other twelve council members murmur among themselves as Kurt and Cory put down their proposals.

"Silence, please. The council is now in session. Scribe, please make a record of the attendees and note the additional presence of our Keeper of the Crystals, Kurt Couric, and our Keeper of the Flames, Cory Tantor."

The chancellor looks around the council, sighs wearily, and continues, "I have invited Cory and Kurt here, or rather, they have invited themselves, because the information they have been collecting over the past few months is rather disturbing and demands our attention. With that said, I give the word to Kurt."

Kurt scans the council members one by one; his face changes from weariness into a welcoming smile. "Dearly beloved ones, I've been receiving numerous visions over the past few months, and they all point to the same outcome. The destruction of the way we live our lives. Cory and I have been journeying beyond the veils to meet with our other selves in different timelines and our guides and master guides who are no longer in physical form, and they confirmed the path we are on. It is time to start making preparations for our departure from the face of the Earth and retreat into Inner Earth, where our ancestors came from."

"That's quite a bold statement," says one of the council members. "And we respect the knowledge of the Keeper of the Crystals and the Keeper of the Flames. Can you show how you got to these conclusions, and then present your best predictions and possible solutions to address these probable massive changes?"

"Let me demonstrate the first vision. I saw a yellow planet being hit by another planet, but the latter planet was red in color. This collision created an explosion to the extent that both planets were destroyed. I saw two firebirds, red and yellow in color, rising from the center of the explosion and combining into a golden Phoenix, which flew into the Dark Void and arose at the other side, which is our Bright Father Sun. The Phoenix landed on planet Earth and re-created humanoid life from its own energy. These humanoid beings were coming in peace at first, but they carried the karmic imprint of planetary destruction. Next in the vision, I saw huge fireworks indicating war or celebration. However, when next I viewed little girls in the arms of their mothers running across the land, I have to conclude it is war rather than celebration. Cory and I checked with the Ancients, and they claimed that our newfound alliance with Atlantis will come to an abrupt ending and that Atlantis will be destroyed. They recommended we recreate Agartha below the Earth's crust to protect ourselves."

"Atlantis destroyed? That seems impossible. It's such a thriving advanced society, especially technologically."

"The Phoenix is the symbol of destruction and rebirth. There is no detail given on how Atlantis will be destroyed, but it is a fact. What happens on a small scale happens on a larger scale. The destruction of Atlantis is a small version of the destruction of a planet. And to continue the propagation of this event at a smaller scale, the Ancients showed a large floating city-vessel, called *Titanic*, being destroyed on its maiden journey as a warning sign for destruction after hubris. Also, the Ancients claim that humanity's multi-stranded DNA will be tempered with to the extent that we lose our connection to Creator, and, as such, we lose our humanity, only to become mere breeding animals. They recommended selecting individuals with genetic backgrounds that can hold higher frequencies and getting all of them to safety underground so their lineage is maintained over the years. On the planet's surface, fights and wars will ensue, and many civilizations will rise and fall. It will be the Age of the Sleeping Giants."

"Can this council enter your mind and that of Cory to see and feel in more detail what you have experienced?"

"Of course. Are you OK with that Cory?"

"Yes, I am."

A group energy gestalt forms between Cory, Kurt, and the council members. Fifteen minutes later, the chancellor sits with mouth wide open.

"Gaia help us! This is unheard-of. We will need to prepare for the next centuries and millennia while we still have our memories intact."

Kurt continues, "We will need way showers on the surface to make sure that the human-like animals don't completely destroy themselves or the planet. And the help of many of our friends in nonphysical form. I'd like to volunteer to be a way shower."

The chancellor rebukes him shortly. "We can't afford to lose one of our greatest visionaries. You're too connected to Creator and too important an asset. Do you realize that you will lose most of your memory of all that you are?"

"It's the only way to make sure these missions become a success. I'll remember in a rather fast amount of time."

"Or get killed in the process. Or worse, kill yourself during the process."

"Then let us build in security protocols and accelerated memory retrieval procedures, as well as interventions from the other side or from here. We can affect ourselves from the past and from the future."

"That is my concern, Keeper. What will happen to you here as you change yourself in the future? And to us, as we are connected to you."

"Cory will be with me all the time."

Cory's eyes light up: "I will? Oh yes . . . I will."

"Let's table this discussion, gentlemen. Whatever resources you need, they are yours. Unless the rest of the council disagrees."

Silence sweeps across the room. Clearly, all the council members are absorbing and processing the information.

"It is settled then, till our next meeting. Next time, please bring a detailed plan and your team members to the council."

"Chancellor, I suggest next time we meet in the Crystal Chamber where we invoke the Flames and the Crystals along with the Ancients and the entire physical and nonphysical team that will be involved in this operation. In addition to hearing the wisdom from the Ancients, the combined consciousness can show us the most probable timelines and what we need to pay attention to."

"Very well. The Crystal Chamber it is. Meeting dismissed!"

THE PRIEST AND THE SHAMAN

HARMONIC UNIVERSE ONE. Twenty-First Century. Planet Earth.

After being pulled out of his body the night before, Elliott wakes up energized and in a great mood, but with lingering thoughts.

"Is this really happening, or am I going crazy? Why did I see ghost faces in front of people at the dance club? Did I really go to Heaven and have a talk with the Big One? Why is this happening to me?"

For three years, Elliott's partner Josie has been begging him to go to church, and the day after being pulled out of his body, Elliott finally shows up at the spiritual center alone. Desperation is a great motivator. He is greeted warmly and settles himself in a chair somewhat in the middle. Elliott notes that the service is very different than what he was used to in his Catholic days: a very happy atmosphere; lots of singing, clapping, dancing, and a great speech. What more do you want to start off your Sunday? Perhaps a Bloody Mary or mimosa serving station?

Afterward, he makes a straight line to one of the priests. "Hey, I need to talk to you about what is going in my life. Do you have a few minutes?"

"Sure," the priest says. "Let's go to the room next door where we can sit down and have a chat."

That room is a big room with a lot of tiny little tables. Many people seem to be talking about the mess in their lives to a whole army of heavenly helpers. Apparently, Elliott is not the only one with issues that week. So he tells the priest a bit about the events from the week before, and the priest looks unfazed. Surprisingly unfazed.

"Am I the only one who finds it a bit odd that there are things going on that can't be scientifically proven?"

The priest replies, "You need to talk to Maria. She is an expert on this matter."

"Who is Maria?"

"She is here. Let me walk you to her."

So they leave the "hall of tables" and walk back down the long hallway. There are still quite some people from the previous mass in the hallway. As they are progressing through the hallway, about twenty yards from the end, they see a woman with long white hair standing there. She turns around, looks Elliott straight in the eyes, and says, "We need to have a talk."

"I'm guessing you're Maria?"

"Yes, I am."

Maria continues, "Justin, can you take care of this lady here? She's is trying to fill out this form. Thank you."

And so Maria and Elliott walk back into the "hall of tables." Maria sits down, crosses her legs, and smiles slyly at him.

"So, any changes lately?"

"Yes, I see floating faces in front of people and sometimes energy around them. I talk to things that I can't see. I was in an energy cloud or Heaven last night, supposedly talking to God, and as I'm sitting here, my hands are shaking and I feel energy shooting outward to you like laser beams. That's it in a nutshell. Any thoughts?"

"Yes, you are sending energy to me. I can feel it. Thank you. I must have needed that."

"You can feel that? So I'm not going crazy?"

"Yes, I can feel that, and no you're not going crazy. This is completely normal."

"Really? Normal?"

"There are a few things I can help you with. I'm a shaman woman. First off, your third eye is wide open like a shining beacon. You need to learn to close that. Second, you need to learn to ground yourself. Let me help you with that for now. Can't have you walking with your head in the clouds all day long."

She walks behind Elliott, places her hands on his shoulders, and within a minute she starts shaking. Elliott thinks, "*Lady, the last thing I need here is a scene. I can see people staring at us. This is embarrassing.*"

And as he holds that thought, he feels a weird sensation in his body, and he starts shaking too. And he can't stop shaking. And he so wanted to stop acting like a shaking Quaker.

"*Great, now we are having an exorcism scene in a church. Check that one off my list of things to do before I die.*"

The meeting with the shaman lady haunts him the entire day, but there is little left to do. So he hangs out with his friends who know something is going on, but can't quite put their finger on it. Or can they?

The next day while driving to work, he hears that same voice from white energy land in his head, but more like a gentle whisper.

"*Corinthians two fourteen.*"

"Great. Now I hear voices in my head when I'm awake. That sounds like a Bible passage though."

Elliott takes the next exit, pulls off the road, and googles the sentence.

"But the natural man does not receive the things of the Spirit of God, for they are foolishness to him; nor can he know them, because they are spiritually discerned," he reads.

"That doesn't help much," Elliott sighs, and he moves on with his workday.

EAGLES AND RAMS

HARMONIC UNIVERSE ONE. Twenty-First Century. Planet Earth.

As Elliott continues to go down his path, he is confronted with what one would call unusual happenings. He starts seeing energy fields around people. Some may call them auras. Or he would see shimmers of silhouettes in the shape of humans. Imagine that you are looking at the hot air right above the desert sand; that's what he means with "shimmering air." But instead of flat and horizontal shimmering air like in the desert, the shimmering air actually has a defined upright humanoid shape and it moves. One night, one of those shimmering figures crawl toward him over the bed while Elliott is having a private moment. The shimmer walks through him to the extent that his whole body turns freezing cold. In a second that happy ending he is looking for vaporizes into a scream of terror.

Of course, his scientific mind needs some invalidation, so he makes an appointment with a psychiatrist. That and a lot of his friends have been gently nudging him to go see a doctor and also check for brain damage. Some friends have been flat out avoiding him or voicing extreme concern about his new developments. Elliott is feeling lonely. Too lonely to be good. Ironically, the first time slot available for the psychiatric session is thirty minutes after his next meeting with Rashelle.

A few days later at Rashelle's practice.

"Rashelle, I have been seeing a ton of eagles and rams this last week. Not real ones, but like in autostereograms. If I stare for a few seconds, a 3-D image of an eagle or a ram pops up in the color, and the print of whatever I'm staring at: granite countertops, floors, pillows, sweaters, etc. In fact, the white sweater you are wearing now, there is a ram head jumping out right now. What does it mean?"

"Well, eagles help you connect with a deity. With regards to the rams, I don't know. My zodiac sign is Aries, and that's a ram. Maybe because I am your mentor?"

The whole meeting goes by quickly, and luckily this time he feels a lot more energy flowing through his body. "*One step closer to figuring out all the secrets of the Universe,*" he muses to himself. He exits quickly because he wants to be on time for his first session with his psychiatrist. Elliott enters the opulent office, sits down, and looks around the gleaming wooden furniture and bundles of books and papers.

Eagles and rams everywhere.

"*Am I in my own version of* The Truman Show*? What is going on here?*"

The session is uneventful, and based on the facts presented, there is nothing much the psychiatrist wants to do.

"Elliott, I don't know what to tell you. There are people who genuinely see and hear things, and there are people who think they see and hear things. If what you say is true, and I see no reason why you would lie about your witness stories, then you might be part of the first category. I'd like to monitor this over time though, but I can't prescribe anything or diagnose you at this point in time."

"Thanks. I'm not sure whether I should be happy about this or not."

FROM COINCIDENCE TO SYNCHRONICITY

HARMONIC UNIVERSE ONE. Twenty-First Century. Planet Earth.

A few weeks after Elliott's noncommittal clearance by the psychiatrist, Elliott's neighbor Danny comes by to visit and brings along his new friend Suma, whom he met at the local coffee shop. Eventually, they come to the topic of Elliott's newfound interest in energy healing. Danny's friend is intrigued and asks if he would do a session with her.

Ten minutes later, Danny leaves, and Elliott takes Suma to the bedroom and asks her to lie down on the bed with her eyes closed while he remains standing at the foot of the bed. Elliott is trying to concentrate on the energy, but little does he know that her little puppy was set on getting to know him a lot better. Imagine how sharp puppy teeth are, and how hard it is to concentrate on energy healing when there is a little monster gnawing at your bare ankles. Luckily, Elliott had just learned how to do healing from a distance. So what better reason to practice distance healing than to evade puppy monster? He climbs on the dark brown wooden dresser across from the bed, too far away to wave his hands over her body. He closes his eyes and focuses on the necessary symbols and intent to do the distance healing. "*Great light show*" is one of his thoughts. Anyhow, it all goes fine, and then he starts getting short visual and auditory messages. He hears the words "*star child*." Then he gets the image of a pentagram, and finally he receives "*crystal wands*" as a mental sound. He tells her about it, but he has no clue what it means, and he doesn't ask for an explanation either. Since the mystery is unlikely to become resolved that night, they both decide to get a refreshing sleep before work in the morning.

The next morning, during meditation, the Creator's voice returns.

"*You're going to die today.*"

"*I'm sorry, what? Did you say I'm going to die today?*"

"*Yes.*"

"*OK, just checking. Hold on. You speak a different language sometimes. Is my physical body going to die?*"

"*No, you're going to kill your ego self.*"

"*Oh, I guess that's OK?*"

"*Yes, it is a good thing.*"

Later that day while shopping for groceries, Elliott runs into a sign that says Tarot Card Reader. He decides to call and make an appointment, even though he is still very skeptical about this metaphysical stuff. But when it comes to dying, he just wants a second opinion. When he arrives at the tarot card reader's practice, the practitioner introduces himself as Timmy and gives his business card, which reads: Timmy Starchild.

"*Wow, what a coincidence,*" Elliott thinks. "Starchild *is the word I got yesterday night.*"

Timmy throws down some rune stones and then asks Elliott to pick five cards from the tarot card deck.

First card: death.

"*Wasn't I going to die today according to Creator?*"

Second card: a person holding a pentagram.

"*Funny, that's the image I got in my head last night. What a coincidence.*"

Third card: a series of crystal wands.

Elliott is now thinking in overdrive. "*Too much coincidence going on here.*"

He notices the three blatant messages from last night and the death message from this morning in one and the same reading. This is no longer coincidence, and then he remembers what his mentor told him. "If you get messages from the other side during a healing, ask them if they are for the other person or for you." Obviously, the messages were all for him, or maybe for both.

Fourth card: the tower.

Fifth card: wheel of fortune.

Timmy commences his explanation.

"The tower indicates that a Divine intervention is shaking your core belief system. The death card can mean transitioning, but what I'm getting is that you are going to kill your ego. You're trying to figure out who you are, and you will have abundance and much help during your journey."

"*Bang! Bang! Bang!*" That's the sound of Elliott killing his scientific ego.

THE ANCIENTS AND THE CRYSTAL CAVE

HARMONIC UNIVERSE TWO. 75,000 BC. Lemuria. Planet Earth.

The entrance to the Crystal Cave is located within the garden of Edana Park at the East side of Stellar City. Lush trees, tropical flowers, ponds, and colorful birds find refuge here. The whole scenery is barely noticed by the council members who are on their way to meet the Keeper of the Flames, Cory Tantor, and the Keeper of the Crystals, Kurt Couric.

"Do we have to get wet these days just to have a meeting?" one of the council members asks. She is adorned with jewelry and is wearing embroidered Lemurian council clothes.

"The only entrance to the Crystal Cave is through the waterfall by the center lake. So yes, there is a great chance you will get wet. All of us will get wet," Chancellor Troy rebukes her.

When they arrive at the waterfall, the sun is bright yellow in color, and its rays are reflected in the clear water of the waterfall, giving the illusion that white, golden light is rushing down into the lake. Each of the council members passes through the waterfall over a jasper stone path, laid out carefully in a pattern that resembles a spiral.

The council enters the Crystal Cave, which has two levels. The first level has a large white crystal round table and many crystal generators attached to the table in a three-by-four pattern. The second level is more like a balcony level with seating or standing room for the councilors, and a silver metal pentagram frame, adorned with a pattern of crystals, hangs from a circular black onyx roof.

When the council members are seated, Kurt addresses the audience.

"Thank you, wise councilmen and councilwomen for being here today to reflect on a plan that lays out the rescue of humanity after the fall of Atlantis. Cory has energized the appropriate flames, and I will activate the crystals soon to create a trans-dimensional secure connection with the Ancients. I don't know who will come through, but I have invited many of them."

Kurt lies down on the white round crystal table surrounded by a multitude of colored flames. Soft fire hues are reflected off the white crystal table and the clear quartz cave walls. Kurt connects with the council members merely by setting his intent and then asks for the Ancients to come forward. A few seconds later, a sudden surge in energy immerses the room. The crystalline generators surrounding the round table light up brightly, and they release their buffer seals to handle the inflow of energy. At the same time, the flames surrounding the round table rise much higher, and the pentagram's crystals light up brightly. Multiple flames in a rainbow of colors appear out of nowhere and hover around and above Kurt's body on the round table.

"Good day, my dearest humans, I am Mika'El, representative for the Elohim Collective from the angelic kingdom." The voice emanates from a golden flame that appears above Kurt.

"And we are the Ra Confederacy, at your service." This voice comes from the red flame above Kurt.

"The Amonites are pleased to be here with you as well," says the blue flame.

"There are many members of star systems from within this time matrix and from outside your physical reality. They are listening in through the other flames. Our collective mind will speak through your visionary as he has allowed us the use of his body during this transmission," says Kurt's body, but his voice sounds much louder and deeper.

"Very well, let's continue. As you are all aware, a major cataclysm will happen about sixty-five thousand years from now. We will intervene by removing the Amanti memory sphere from your planet's core in order to prevent the destruction of this construct. The Amanti sphere holds the memory for the evolution and for the mass consciousness of your species. Its removal from the planet's core will result in memory loss of all humans who have not assembled their first five strands of DNA. Those who will have assembled their first five DNA strands will be taught how to pass through a series of dimensional portals, which we call the Halls of Amanti. Through this network of dimensional portals they can link to the Amanti memory sphere and into the power core that brings life to your entire planet. The Amanti memory sphere will be placed at an undisclosed location in the Dal Universe."

"That sounds like a lot of work. Can't you just prevent the cataclysm?" says the chancellor.

"The cataclysm is a direct result from the exertion of free will by extraterrestrial entities who do not wish your species to evolve to its Divine destiny. We have little power over free will per the decree of Prime Creator. Before circumventing free will, we first have to exhaust all other options."

The chancellor inquires carefully, "What happens to the people who did not evolve far enough to assemble their first five strands? Some Souls will barely have reincarnated here on Earth. Asking them to assemble all of the first five strands through life experience is a bit much, don't you think?"

"That is a long story, and it depends on each individual Soul which chooses its own path with Prime Creator. Not having assembled all strands does not mean inferior, because we are all equal. It just means on a different path like choosing to eat a cookie versus choosing to eat an apple. That's why we want you to focus on the big picture. Because what happens on Earth will affect many systems in the galaxy. Remember one of the Hermetic principles: 'As above so below, as below so above.' Soon after the cataclysm on Earth, human societies will need to be rebuilt. We will be forced to place a barrier around the planet, and this will eventually result in a separation of the lower, the middle, and the higher self in terms of experiencing consciousness. The biggest development here will be the rise of the ego mind."

"What is an ego mind?" asks the council member of wisdom.

"An ego mind is embodied within the physical and the mental body, and it experiences itself as separate when two individuals physically perceive one another. As a consequence, it needs to prove itself or its existence out of feeling superior or not feeling deserving or not feeling unconditional love. The unconditional love is experienced by the Divine Self-consciousness, which will be unable to communicate directly with the ego mind for quite a long time. The middle self will serve as a mediator to communicate in between both during the dream state. In short, one being will have three dimensional planes that it experiences simultaneously. The ego mind will be the most isolated of these three personalities."

The council member of wisdom is baffled.

"How can we be separate from one another? I see myself in the other. That is quite simple to understand, no?"

And the answer follows through Kurt's body.

"Apparently not when you are in ego mind mode. Allow me to continue with a proposed agenda. The Ra Confederacy will start the groundwork by sending Ishtar and her family to the Sumerian and Babylonian regions. They will be known as Gods, because of the knowledge and the technology they will have access to. After Babylonia, Egypt will rise as a nation of Gods. In order to remind humanity of the Sacred Law of One, the Ra Confederacy will be sending one advanced Soul along with thousands of support troops. He will be known as Pharaoh Akhenaton, and he will reintroduce the Sacred Law of One to humanity. Power struggles during the reign of Akhenaton could be a result, and there are highly probable timelines where the influence of the ego mind and its ensuing interindividual power struggle will lead to a contamination of the Amanti memory sphere. This contamination will force us to seal off access to the higher realms for those Souls who were involved in this unfortunate event, and, as such, they will be placed under the so-called Templar seals. It will be talked about as the 666 curse. Earth will be quarantined for a long time, and humanity will need to evolve on its own. If the contamination occurs, we will have to withdraw many advanced technologies from the Earth's surface, such as the Ankh's and the crystal generators, because humanity and its leadership will have then proven themselves irresponsible when it comes to the use of technologies that they barely understand. Only Inner Earth will have access to these technologies. It will become more difficult to manipulate matter and to rebuild cities and monuments like pyramids and temples. After thousands of years, the Egyptian dynasty will fall by covert infiltration and subsequent misguidance by Annunaki extraterrestrials. Progress for humanity will slow down tremendously when these technologies have been withdrawn, and instead, many teachers and messengers will be sent. During and after Egypt, the brunt of the work will be handed over to the Elohim, who will communicate through figures like the Greek philosophers Plato and Socrates and through so-called angelic visits to the founding fathers of new religions and sciences. The Greek society will become the second cradle of civilization, and that center will move to a city more west of Greece, called Rome. This society will become mainly patriarchal, and limited interaction between the Ancients and that civilization will occur because of their embrace of distorted teachings of the Law of One. During the Roman times, in Jerusalem, an Elohim twelfth-level avatar will be born and by way of its Soul birth through the Amanti memory sphere, the original blueprint of the sphere will be restored. As such, he could be considered the savior of all the descendants that carry the Templar seal that is genetically carried forward from the Egyptian times. He will be known as Jeshua or Jesus. The twelfth-level avatar's life will be at risk, and he will be spared an untimely death. Instead, a volunteer will take his place in exchange for accelerated Soul growth. The bloodline of the twelfth-level avatar will be maintained and kept secret for their own protection. These descendants will carry through their advanced DNA higher frequencies into the physical realities, and they will, quite literally, be the lifelines of Creator energy into that physical reality. The volunteer taking Jeshua's place at the cross will be born again about two millennia later to meet and connect all timelines as a way to demonstrate the Law of One in action across many Universes. Much obscurity and confusion exists around these timelines, so not everything is set in stone.

"The Amonites will work through most of Western civilization and will have a strong base at the island of Avalon. Meantime, the Edonites are placing representatives in isolated areas of the world as a redundancy option to the destruction of most civilized human societies, which is a probable future as well. The Nordic regions will be visited by so-called Asgardians, while the Melchizedek line will establish settlements in Middle- to South-America to balance Annunaki infiltration. The Sirian Council has agreed to contact and teach the Hopi Indians as well as isolated tribes in Africa. The Orion Council has agreed to make landings and teachings in Australia. The Ra Confederacy will work through Confucius and the Taoists in the East. The Vishnu aspect of the Ra Confederacy will send many avatars spread out over time, which will be known as Buddha, Krishna, and the like."

"Africa, Australia, America? So many names. This is confusing," says the Chancellor.

"Those three names are continents, huge landmasses so to speak. The shape of the world and its naming will look different than what it is now, and that is why we contacted your seer, Kurt, so you can start preparing. You can see this as a game, but let me tell you, the way you experience the game is up to you. Do you want to be proactive and be prepared or let things happen as they come? Neither approach is invalid or less than the other. We are just informing you what will likely happen based on the probabilities in timelines that we see. The highest probabilities that we see may not be what transpires in the consciousness of mass awareness. There are many alternatives that may or may not transpire in terms of probabilities in the parallelistic Universe. In most timelines, Earth is destroyed, and that is why we are asking you to prepare as many of your people over the next sixty-five thousand years to accelerate and live beneath the surface, because these timelines carry the most chance of survival and fulfilling your Soul contract."

"What about the intruders?"

"There are many, and they will distort the Sacred Teachings of the Law of One wherever they can. If in a teaching, you do not see unconditional love for each other, no matter who you are or what you do, or if you see segregation or categorization with favoritism, then you must be cautious and apply your own discernment. That teaching is circumspect to the Law of the Most High Love, and yet, it could be an aspect of it. There are very little 'yes and no' answers in this Universe. It usually depends on perspective. Your perpetrators will use the ego mind to entice society and individuals further into their destruction, and they will not even see it coming. Even worse, some of these groups will be thinking they are following the Divine, where, in fact, they are following an extraterrestrial being who proclaims to be their God and whose agenda is to enslave them for eternity. To not live your life as a Divine being, to live as a slave to a system that was instilled by outside forces as the only reality is an atrocity according to our identity aspects, but out of unconditional love, we have to let both sides play their games. What your future suppressors don't seem to realize is that they will reincarnate as the ones being oppressed so that the Souls can learn the lessons from both sides. Also, your future selves, at least the ones who survived, have agreed to come to assist humanity. Many Pleiadian and Arcturian forces have agreed to come to Earth through reincarnation or through armadas of support starships and star bases. Kurt's past self is a

Pleiadian in training for his mission as a commander, which is millions of years in the future from now. With regards to Cory . . ."

The cave goes dark for a few seconds, and then low lighting emitted from the table-sized crystals sends a blue hue across the crystal cave. Kurt slowly gets up from the crystal table and stumbles, speaking in an unsteady voice.

"We lost connection. The crystals need to be recharged again before we can set up another trans-dimensional meeting. May I suggest that we sojourn to digest this information? We can reassemble at a later time frame."

"That would be wise, Kurt. We have a lot to think about. I'll contact you later to set up the next meeting."

IMPERFECT PERFECTION

HARMONIC UNIVERSE ONE. Twenty-First Century. Planet Earth.

After a few productive weeks, Elliott visits a local festival and meets a new person who is handing out wristbands to enter the grounds. In the meantime, Josie has returned from Brazil, and she is still not fully on board with all the strange events that seem to be happening left and right. The person who is handing out wristbands is named Miley, and she smiles profusely. She is as chatty as Elliott, and they are quite the social butterflies together. Suddenly Creator's voice thunders in his head again.

"Ask her about her rape when she was eight years old."

"Dude, that's not how we do it here on Earth. I just met her. And what is up with that anyway?"

"Well, it would really help her to talk about it."

Elliott's scientific mind comes online again and sees an ideal opportunity. That portion of his mind is still wondering what is going on, even though it is less prominent after Elliott's visit with the tarot card reader.

"*Wait a minute,*" says his scientific mind. *"Paranoia and psychosis are internal realities that are projected outward to be perceived real. But this is a real person, and I have Josie here as a witness. They both look normal and physical. Let's test this out!"*

So Elliott musters all his courage, and in a diplomatic-sounding tone, he says, "Miley, don't take this the wrong way, but have you ever been raped when you were eight years old?"

Josie's eyes fly wide open, and she stares at him bewildered, wondering why her boyfriend would say something so unconventional and out of the blue. It definitely doesn't sound like the old Elliott. On the other hand, Miley's eyes are filling with tears, and in a quivering voice she says, "Yes. How do you know that?"

Elliott mutters, "——t, ——t, ——t, this is really happening. Oh my God. For real."

And while his mind is processing this newfound information, he utters, "I hear this voice in my head, and it said that you could benefit from talking about it."

"This is too weird, Elliott," says Josie, and she walks to the beer stand where the rest of their friends are hanging out.

Miley is smiling timidly now and continues.

"So you're an angel like me?"

"I guess so. I don't really know who or what I am. But I've had some interesting experiences to say the least, like being pulled from my body into Heaven."

"Maybe we can compare notes. I had a near-death experience when I was very young. I saw my body lying dead on the ground and then moved to the white light. When I was surrounded by white light, I received many instructions, and then I was returned to my body, which was healed. You were on the other side too?"

"Yes, I was. But I didn't die though, or at least I think I didn't die. I had a great conversation with a very benevolent, patient, and wise being. Apparently, I am a messenger."

"You're just starting to remember who you are. You're in for quite a ride. Call me anytime if you want to catch up. I need to help my team here with the wristbands. Bye!"

Later that night, Elliott is getting prepared in his bedroom for meditation. When he lies down, he feels a presence, but unlike the Creator.

"*Who is here?*" he asks while reaching out with his mind.

"I have come to teach you, Elliott. I am one of your guides. In fact, I am one of your guardian angels."

"I have guardian angels?"

"Everybody does. You have four guardian angels: Archangel Metatron, Archangel Uriel, Archangel Gabriel, and myself Archangel Michael."

"All my guides are archangels?"

"No, you have many other guides, and some will change over time as you remember what you need to remember. At this space/time coordinate, you have as guides Theseus, Socrates, Plato, Mother Mary (also known as Shakti), Ganesh (also known as Thoth), Jesus Christ, the Red Dragon, Pegasus, and your Pleiadian sister Kayla and her team, and you will meet others over time. Each is ready to serve you, and they understand that you need time to work with them."

"Wow! That's a lot of guides. What do I do with them?"

"Just call them forward or invoke them the same way you call forward the Creator of all that is. We are merely aspects of the One, just like you are, and in that sense you and I are the same."

"Does that mean I have to be perfect?"

"Elliott, you didn't come here to be perfect. The majority of you is perfect on 'the other side', as you call it, perfect in the way that you define it. However, you came forward in this physical reality to experience contrast and to be imperfect. You are perfectly imperfect."

"So I can do whatever I want?"

"Yes, do what you want to do when you want to do it, with an open heart, not an ego mind. You're exploring desires right now, and that will change as you have satisfied your desires and move on to the next. Do not become a slave of your desires. Merely see them as a tool to create who you are and who you want to be. First accept and embrace yourself totally. The light and the dark side are both part of you—the good and the bad. When you know who you are and you unconditionally love your desirable and non-desirable attributes, then in an attitude of non-discrimination you can decide to redefine yourself and decide that a certain attribute, let's say arrogance, is no longer wanted, and as such, you have defined it as a nonself. The Universe will then bring you opportunities to allow you to express the release of this attribute and the appearance of its counter-attribute, humility. It almost becomes a challenge to test whether you really don't want this anymore. It's almost like the Universe is asking: "Are you really sure you want to let this go?" It is important to learn this now and become better at it because there will come a time when your thoughts and emotions become manifest much quicker than they do now, so you need to build up your foundation of self to work from."

"What about doing bad things?"

"From the perspective of the infinite, there is no good or bad. There just is. We want what you want. Unconditional love, remember? What bad things are you referring to?"

"For instance, people who do drugs."

"Matter does not exist in the absolute, and it exists only in the relative. In fact, look at time like a molten lava stream cooling in the ocean. It gets stuck for a bit after solidifying, and when the pressure from the in-flowing lava gets too high, then the lava tube protrudes out just a little farther and solidifies again. That is, one can see the Universe develop. Watch again the movie Prometheus *and see how the attending officer is mulling through the memories of the humans who are kept in stasis. The way he skips through her lifetime memories is how we look at your life. We notice your cries for help or attention by a strong emotion or with a single focused thought or a ritual or a combination thereof. These are registered energy patterns within the space/time matrix that we can easily pick up and pay attention to even if they already happened, and if help is needed, we program in the right code and voila, the miracle happens, whether it gets noticed or not. We strive to stay in the background because you would grow dependent on us, and we want you to live your own life. In your case, you are eager to learn, and so we come to your assistance rather easily because we know that you will utilize this knowledge for the greater good. To further answer your question about drugs: remember the lava analogy? Well if you go from un-protruded to newly protruded magma fragment, you could imagine that there is a 'time lag' in between those two configurations. And matter does not exist in between the moments (in the absolute). This is carefully explained by one of your early twentieth-century physicists Dr. Heisenberg and correctly assumed by Dr. Einstein: "Matter does not exist the way most people think it exists." Second, matter is merely a translation of energy frequency patterns through a morphogenetic field from the Unified Field, so you have the option to decide how the matter will influence you. If you do nothing with the ingested substance then your bodies' functions will succumb to the frequency pattern of the substance. You could also decide to transmute the frequency pattern of a substance and literally change its properties. Mystics in your reality call this transmutation, and the clearest example of that is still being utilized in Christian churches as the breaking of the bread and the pouring of the wine. That is what Jesus did. He put his single thought-focused mind into the frequency patterns and altered the pattern so that it would create a different effect, and His intended effect was*

to link His energies with that of His disciples and their descendants. You can do the same thing with drugs if you really want to. In that case, the effects of taking a drug will be different after their transmutation. Second, from our perspective and assuming that you do not transmute the frequencies of a drug that you are about to ingest, it is not wrong to experience the effects of ingesting a so-called drug substance. From a narrow human mind-set we can see how that can become an issue, but that person's Soul may have decided that ingesting this or that substance is beneficial for the individual's human experience. Who are you to judge?"

"But it kills people and ruins their life?"

"Is that so? Then, so it is as you declare it. Or consider that there are lessons to be learned here for both the people judging the users and for the users avoiding contempt or isolation or embracing peer pressure or just plainly enjoying the moment. It is different for every person, but it is not up to you, nor I, to judge this or that behavior as invalid."

"What if their behavior kills other people, like drunk driving?"

"My dear Elliott, you and many of your fellow human beings still live under the illusion that everything is under the control of your ego, and your ego desperately wants to believe that. Everything happens for a reason, and all is in perfect balance at any given moment. Do you honestly think that a force that created you could not recreate you and make you forget in the highly unlikely case that something unanticipated would happen? You have died many times in this current human experience, just like most people. For example, we rebuilt your body the night you were driving from Brussels to Antwerp, and you lost control over the vehicle on the slippery highway roads. It was not in your plan to die that night, so you were rebuilt. Others may have made the decision to exit their human life experience through a car accident or peacefully in their sleep. It depends on many decisions at many different planes of existence."

"I didn't die that night. I ended up on a patch of grass facing the direction I came from."

"And how did you get there?"

"I don't know. I blanked when I started skidding off the highway."

"Yes, you blanked. In reality, you skidded off the road, and we had to put your body and your car back in good condition enough for you to get home. We erased your memory of what happened, so you wouldn't wonder how you got so lucky. We left you some memory so you can put one and one together. You skidded off on the right side of the road, right?"

"I was in the process of moving to the right side of the road, and then I blanked, yes."

"Where was the patch of grass?"

"On the left side."

"Now put one and one together. How can you end up on the left side of a three-lane road on an elevated patch of grass when you lost all control going over the right lane, and how come you remember that little detail only now and not when you woke up behind the wheel from your ordeal?"

"Holy crap. This was all orchestrated?"

"You, and everyone else, are so taken care of it is beyond your imagination. The Universe is like a reverse casino. It's all in your favor, because we want you to have the best experience ever."

"Then why are most people having a miserable life?"

"That, I will answer another time. Now process this information and put it to good use if you want. You are much loved by many beings."

THE DANCE FLOOR BECOMES THE CLASSROOM

HARMONIC UNIVERSE ONE. Twenty-First Century. Planet Earth.

Elliot, Josie, and their friends congregate at Jeff's house before going to the nightclub. Jeff cannot find his wallet, and obviously he can't go with them unless he is able to locate the holder of his identity card. All of them are frantically searching the house to no avail. So Elliott silently asks Creator for the location of the wallet, and he hears a soft mental whisper: "*It's in the bedroom.*" Elliott decides to tell them, and of course, the rest of the gang not being on board with his newfound spiritual development doesn't really pay much attention to the new information. Jeff traces back his steps from earlier in the day to the ATM where he withdrew money, but there is no wallet there either. In the end, Jeff decides to stay home. Beckster, Reed, Josie, and Elliott leave for the dance club.

On the dance floor, Beckster shouts out, "Jeff found his wallet! He's coming over."

"Where was it?" asks Elliott.

"In the bedroom, but he doesn't want to tell you because that means you were right about what you heard in your crazy head. You didn't hear it from me," Beckster says.

They have a great night dancing, and suddenly Elliott sees Archangel Michael towering over the whole dance floor, about three hundred feet high. His message carries a different vibration or tone than the Creator, and the archangel starts teaching.

"*Stay within yourself. Do not venture outside of you. Consider your eyes windows to a virtual reality. Be grateful for what comes, and then let it go and detach. Savor the experience, but do not get attached to it.*"

The whole team of friends decides to leave after one more song. Elliott looks up at Archangel Michael. "*This last dance is for you.*" And he starts dancing his ass off. No thoughts whatsoever, just plain getting into the music and flowing with it. And then, he senses the entire cosmos inside him, and he is looking through his eyes as if they were windows; he sees all the people and his friends laughing and dancing. They seem to be at a distance, and he is happy for them, feeling connected and fully detached at the same time.

"*It is so clear in the moment,*" Elliott thinks. "*I have seen myself and others looking for things and persons to complete ourselves and find happiness. But real happiness comes from within, and we don't need anything to complete ourselves because we are perfect in our incompleteness and ever expanding through our experiences. There is nothing we have to do to prove ourselves or to please others. The fact that we are here is evidence that we are all worthy, and we are here for a reason and not by accident. And that reason is very simple: to find out who we are through the experience of living and the thoughts, words, and actions that we choose. Life is what we make it. I am not from this world, but I choose to live in it. And it's awesome!*"

CONFIDENCE AND ASCENSION

HARMONIC UNIVERSE ONE. Twenty-First Century. Planet Earth.

Josie is getting more and more on board with Elliott's newfound spirituality, and she has seen him perform quite a few miraculous healings on people. When Josie returns to Brazil, she visits one of her friends who is in dire need of help or energy healing. Josie decides to call Elliott from Brazil to perform a healing from a distance for this particular friend who is having a really hard time. During that healing, Elliott receives a message related to confidence issues, and since he has learned that in a lot of cases, messages are meant for both the patient and the healer, he reaches out to Creator after the healing session.

"Creator, do I still have confidence issues?"

"*Yes, you do*," replies Creator.

"Ugh," Elliott sighs.

A few hours later, Elliott goes shopping with his friend Beckster for a meaningful necklace to go with his Halloween outfit for a dance party in Los Angeles. The lady who works at the counter addresses them in a very friendly tone.

"What are you looking for?"

"A necklace for my Halloween outfit," Elliott replies.

"Oh! OK, what is your outfit going to be?"

"A warlock. I'll paint these symbols on my body and I need a necklace to go with it. I'll call my dark self for that night, John Darko."

She squints her eyes and speaks softly, "You know, I make necklaces based on your aura."

"Really? What does my aura tell you?" asks Elliott suspiciously.

She looks at him, through him, and around him.

"Hm. Interesting aura. Quite beautiful to watch. There it is. You need more confidence."

"Oh my God," Elliott gasps. "I heard that a few hours ago from a guy that's too smart for his own good, wings and all."

Needless to say he asks her to make the necklace.

Later that night, the gang goes out dancing, and about one hour in, Elliott feels a presence entering. It almost feels like a large hammer falling down on a wooden floor. He searches with his consciousness to see what's going on, and it's got that alpha male presence, unmistakably Archangel Michael.

Elliott reaches out with his mind: "*Michael?*"

"*Yes.*"

"*Are you here for me?*"

"*Yes, I am, Elliott. You wanted to learn about confidence. Who better to learn from than myself, Archangel Michael? Are you ready?*"

"*Sure. Michael, can I keep dancing?*"

"*Yes, you can, and yes, you may if you so desire. Now take a look at that girl over there. Does she look confident to you?*"

"*I don't think so, Michael. She looks rather shy and timid.*"

"*Correct. How about the other guy over there? Does he have confidence?*"

"*That one? With the blue shirt? He looks rather confident to me.*"

"*Not really, Elliott. The energy underlying his demeanor is arrogance, not confidence. Arrogance and timidity are two symptoms of the same problem, lack of confidence.*"

"*Then how do I get more confidence?*" sighs Elliott.

"*It is very simple. First, it is not a matter of getting more confidence. It is a matter of losing confidence. Look at every person as if it was yourself. And in absolute reality that is true. The minute you judge anyone for any reason whatsoever—too small, too tall, not enough money, not smart enough, etc.—you are basically judging yourself and that is how you lose your confidence. It is not about getting more confidence. You are giving it away when you look for validation or invalidation outside.*"

"*Wow. That is simple. How did I not come up with that one?*"

"*We are not done yet, young one. Are you ready for a download?*"

Pensively, Elliott replies, "*I guess so.*"

A hint of concern comes through a warning from Archangel Michael.

"You may want to get off the dance floor for this."

And Elliott confidently throws his hands up in the air to the beat of the music while mentally responding, *"Uhm, I would rather stay here."*

"As you wish."

And then the information pours in. It is too much for Elliott to handle, and he has to get off the dance floor.

His friend Jeff notices and shouts in his ear.

"Are you OK?"

"Give me a few minutes downtime. I'll be back soon," Elliott utters distractedly, and he walks off the dance floor. He whips out his phone and starts making notes to the best of his abilities. Besides the vast amounts of energetic data coming in, he is able to receive and write down some mental communication.

"Not all believers are believers. This is not a game of waiting and believing. Those who feel ready would do well to invite in the light for ascension. The light starts building the other DNA strands. Each group of twelve has unique group sequences, and each individual in the group carries its own unique personal sequence. There are twelve-by-twelve groups needed for ascension of humanity."

"That's only one hundred and forty-four people?"

"No, a lot more. Millions, but always in groups of twelve-by-twelve. Aliens are around to assist you. Call on them."

"When is this ascension going to happen?"

"It has already started. It is a gradual process, and it will take five to ten years to complete in this timeline. Find others who are awake. You need to purify yourself first. Everybody has to do this for themselves, and much assistance is provided and needs to be actively asked for. Call for help and guidance for even the smallest things. It is our joy to assist you, because you and I are the same. Be open, make your own self, and have fun!"

"What about work?"

"Your thoughts create your reality. Work is irrelevant from our perspective. Only joy. Ask, and it shall be given."

"How many will ascend?"

"It is Prime Creator's wish that all ascend. The experiment where enlightenment leads to a disappearance from this physical reality has already been experienced, and only a very small percentage of humanity is able to fully ascend. The others remain behind because of genetic blocks, seals, frequency fences, and meddling by unenlightened aliens. The current

experiment is different. In this experiment, you and many others were sent as antennas for ultrahigh frequencies, which then passively or actively transmit into your environment. If you and your brothers and sisters would not be here, those ultrahigh frequencies would pass straight through Earth, and this planet would perish. Trust me. That reality exists. Which one do you want to experience? When you set your intent to transmitting the UHF energies and perform these ceremonies in a group setting, this carries even more acceleration, like putting your foot on the gas pedal. Imagine that the Earth is a boy living in a plastic room with no oxygen supply. The little boy would die of oxygen deprivation in less than a few hours. You, and many others, are the rescue team coming in with hoses attached to your gear that are linked to an oxygen pump. Your presence pumps oxygen in the plastic room. The time frame for Earth's ascension is not hours, but years or decades at your current space/time coordinate. There are those who wish you and your brothers and sisters harm, because you are different. Yet, it is our differences and our similarities that unite us. Diversity is a strength. Just look at your ecosystems.

"To the ones who came to prevent humanity's Grand Awakening, I say that if that is what you want to experience, you will receive it. But we will decouple the fate of humanity from your experience to allow you to experience that reality out of unconditional love. Know that with the intention that you move forward, so will it be that you are treated. Nobody is judged on their belief system, because you all work with a limited and different set of experiential data. The belief system that you hold will be applied to you so that through experience you can learn and adapt your beliefs as you see fit. Eventually, you will discover the Sacred Law of One and act knowingly and anticipate the consequences of your intentions, thoughts, and actions. Do not force your beliefs on anyone else's. If you believe it is OK to subdue an entire species, whether they are humans or animals, then so it will be that your species is subdued. In fact, you are creating your own future. Yes, humanity evolved fast to the extent that they grew strong enough to harm you and your loved ones. Instead of wiping out the human race, do you not see that you are creating the future humans? It is not too late to reconcile and change course unless that is what you want to experience."

Archangel Michael continues teaching. "*Elliott, you are here to wake up people so that we all come to the realization that the One is All, We are All, and We are One. And we are literally One Being. If you do harm to another individual, you are, in fact, hurting yourself twice. Once because the other individual is you. Twice because the Law of Cause and Effect, also known as the Law of Reciprocity, will come into play and what you put out, you also get back. So next time you get all up in arms over how someone is doing I-don't-care-what-it-is to you, I'd suggest to think twice and consider how you would want to be treated if the situation were reversed knowing what you know now. Also consider that the other may still be ignorant about what you just learned and deserves compassion instead. It will also serve you to remember that not only actions, but also words, thoughts, and especially intent have creative power and fall under the Law of Reciprocity."*

Elliott interrupts Archangel Michael.

"*That is a lot to absorb. Are you talking to me or to others?*"

"*I am talking to both. Your thoughts and my current thought patterns are not as private as you think. It serves for all of us to hear these words. I will leave you to enjoy your time with your friends on the dance floor. I'll keep a portion of my focused conscience around in case you need me. Many blessings and much love.*"

And with that, Elliott returns to the dance floor where Jeff corners him.

"Who are you talking to? Are you talking to yourself again or some imaginary angels? Try not to act crazy when we are out together. People start asking questions whether you are all right in the head. OK?"

Elliott is slightly bummed with that comment.

"I'll try, but I'm not sure if I can make that promise forever."

And the inviting beat of techno music draws them into an illusion of sweaty bodies, expectations, and opportunities. All worries and doubts cease to exist for just a few more hours, and the world just keeps on spinning.

COMING OUT

TELLING FRIENDS WHAT is happening to him is difficult for Elliot. Rather insulting comments, like "Have you seen a doctor lately?" do much damage to Elliott's sharing experience. It's like bringing an expensive bottle of wine to friends and then being told that they would rather drink Bud Light beer. One cannot imagine how much that hurts him, especially because there is still a hint of doubt left whether this is really happening. So on the one hand, he has wonderful experiences, meditations, teachings, feelings with a whole world of new friends who love him unconditionally and who support all that he does, even when he judges some of his choices as poorly made. They always come back and say that it is unproductive to judge yourself in terms of experiencing the most joy. Just move on to the next experience and let the past go completely. The only thing that is real is now, they would say. The past is gone and the future is not yet. So to feel this love from beings that he cannot see with his physical eyes or hear with his physical ears, only with his mind when he is in a meditative state of mind, and on the other hand, to see virtually all his acquaintances, including his best friends, condemn these new experiences as psychotic, boring, or just plain rubbish is very hard on Elliott's psyche. Elliott renounced all religion or God-like affiliations after being raised Catholic. Instead, he decided early on to immerse himself in the comfort of pure logic and scientific evidence. Possibly, Elliott is now reliving the pain and fear of abandonment. Many nights he cries himself to sleep, knowing that his nonphysical all-loving friends and mentors are standing by, offering sweet words of encouragement, but with all their might and knowledge, they are unable to give him the experience of being held by a loving, warm, soothing, and understanding human presence.

One day, one of his best customers, Rory, asks him where all these positive changes in the way he walks and talks come from. Elliott decides to gently open the topic with him.

"Well, I've been going through some changes. It's very enlightening."

"What kind of changes?"

"Well, you are going to find this hard to believe, but I'm talking to a higher being and once in a while Archangel Michael among others. There is a lot more going on than our five senses can perceive, you know?"

"It's about time, Elliott!"

"What do you mean?"

"Elliott, we have reincarnated together so many times and you always forget, and I have to wait a long time until you start remembering. I have known since the minute I met you twelve years ago. Now that you are awakening, I have work to do."

"Hold on, Rory, why have you not told me twelve years ago?"

"Because you wouldn't have believed me."

"I probably would not have. But wait a minute. How do I know you are not just pulling a prank on me? I know you can be a prankster. Let's see if you know this? Archangel Michael told me how to transfer sequences between individuals, so if what you say is true, detail that process to me."

"Do not mess with me, Elliott. I am way older than you." And Rory continues to describe the entire process correctly.

"So, Rory, this is really happening?"

"Yes, it is. Enjoy the ride and hold on tight. That is all I can say."

IT'S HARD TO MAKE IT EASY

HARMONIC UNIVERSE ONE. Twenty-First Century. Planet Earth.

Elliott decides to test the principles of the holographic Universe and asks for success at work. More specifically, he requests an easy sale of one of the highly priced imaging devices that his company sells to scientific researchers that want to quantify DNA or protein in their samples. The next morning, Elliott receives a call from an unknown customer who somehow has gotten his information. The customer wants him to come demonstrate one of his top-of-the line imaging devices. So Elliott goes to demonstrate the machine and guess what, the darn camera does not work.

So when the camera isn't working, our dearest Elliott links up with the other side mentally.

"*Hey, I asked for an easy sale. You are making this hard. WTF?*"

Creator responds in turn. "*Elliott, you need to learn to trust me. Just go home and do nothing.*"

"*Do nothing? I have five researchers here looking like they are definitely not going to buy this pricy instrument. I have competition coming in tomorrow to show their instrument, and at the moment it looks like they are going to get the sale.*"

Patiently Creator answers, "*I know you want to call technical support, the service engineers, and all of your colleagues to replace the camera, but trust me. Do nothing. Go home. Call off the demo and say you will be back soon.*"

Elliott returns to his customers and mumbles an apology with a promise to come back soon. He leaves the building, and when he arrives at home he sees a message from another customer who resides in a different building but at the same company he visited earlier.

"Elliott, we received your special imaging device, but we do not have a computer available yet through our IT department. Can we postpone installing the device till our computer arrives? Joe Smith."

Elliott calls back Joe.

"This is Joe Smith."

"Hi, Joe, it is Elliott."

"Oh, hey, Elliott, I just sent you a message."

"Yes, about that, we can postpone the installation until your computer arrives. No problem. And while I have you on the phone, do you mind if I borrow your camera that came with the instrument? It is for building five, and they are colleagues of yours. My camera does not seem to work, and it would really help me out."

Joe responds amicably. "Sure, no problem. Come pick it up on Monday at 10:00 a.m."

Smiling, Elliott replies, "All right, that's great. Thank you. I'll see on Monday. Bye."

Elliott whispers, "Thank you, Creator!"

Monday morning comes and Elliott is present and ready at 10:00 a.m. However, Joe is not available, and Elliott cannot pick up the camera after all. This annoys Elliott and he sends a message to Creator.

"*Hey, you up there. Come on dude. This isn't fair. I said easy sale. Where is my easy sale?*"

"*You really need to learn to trust me, Elliott. It's already taken care of. Just go home and do nothing.*"

"*You better be right. I'm used to fixing things, not waiting for things to be fixed.*"

"*I know. That is why you need to learn this lesson. Balance in giving and receiving. Balance in everything. You are a giver, and you need to learn to receive without expectations.*"

So Elliott goes home, and later that day, Elliott gets a call from Joe. "Hey, Elliott, I'm really sorry I missed our meeting. Things got really hectic here, but I have talked to the researcher who wanted to see your imager in action, and you don't need to pick up the camera or do the demo. They are just going to purchase it. You should see the order tomorrow morning."

And Elliott hears Creator in his mind. "*There's your easy sale. Now do you trust me?*"

"*Thank you, Creator!*"

LEARNING TO TRUST IN THE CASINO

HARMONIC UNIVERSE ONE. Twenty-First Century. Planet Earth.

The relationship between Elliot and Creator improves every day, and the communication is getting better and better. One day, Elliott sees the number ninety appear left and right, on bills, on license plates, in e-mails, and in random conversations, and he hears "ninety" in a song on the radio. So he decides to ask Creator what it means: "*Creator, what does the number ninety mean?*"

"*You'll find your answer at the casino.*"

"*You want me to gamble? For real?*"

"*Yes. Go for it.*"

"*You're joking, right?*"

"*No, I am not. There is much to gain in the casino.*" This is followed by a thundering laugh.

So Elliott decides to drive to the casino, which was forty-five miles away, which in total would be ninety miles. The mystery continues but remains elusive to Elliott.

While in the casino, Elliott sits down at a twenty-five-cent slot machine and puts in twenty dollars. After excruciatingly long minutes and not a single win, Elliott is closer to zero dollars rather than the much anticipated thirty-three-million-dollar jackpot. Frustration kicks in.

"*Creator, what is going on here? Where is my money? This is not much fun. I drove forty-five miles to lose money?*"

"*As I explained before, Elliott, the reality you live now is a product of what you were thinking before. Set your intent and focus on that single thought for as long as you can, and you will get what you want.*"

Elliott transmits in an upset mental tone: "*Fine, I'll set my intent. I will win the 'Wheel of Fortune' before this drink is over. If not, I am going home.*"

And he loses a few times more until it is down to the last three credits and the last sip. He takes the sip, hits the "play all credits" button, and starts sliding off the chair.

"Bing! Bing! Bing! Wheel . . . of . . . Fortune!"

The wheel starts spinning at the top of the machine, and he receives fifty more credits.

"*OK. I trust you. But I'm still losing seven dollars and fifty cents. Why not let me win more?*"

"*Go play the roulette, and you will make it up there.*"

"*I don't know how to play roulette.*"

"*Just do it, or not. You have free will, so it is up to you.*"

Elliott walks around the casino, intent on finding the roulette tables amidst an inviting chaos of bells ringing and video slot tunes. He finally sits down at one of the roulette tables and forks over sixty dollars in exchange for gambling chips. He is ready to win back his money.

"*Creator, where do I put the chips?*"

"*Elliott, you overanalyze everything. It doesn't really matter. Just put them anywhere.*" And he wins three times in a row until the annoying losing part kicks in. Almost to the extent where he is close to being out of money again. So Elliott links up with his mind.

"*Hey, up there, can I get a little help here, please?*"

"*My dear Elliott, Your first lesson was trust. Your second lesson is cooperativity. You have to learn to be cooperative. Wait until the other players place their chips and then put your chips on the highest stacks.*"

So Elliott waits until most chips have been placed and then places his chips on top of the highest stacks. And surprisingly, the numbers with the highest stacks keep winning for quite a while. All players are making money, and the atmosphere at the table is very amicable to say the least. Gambling is fun when you have a Creator whispering in your ears. But alas, the losing streak kicks in again. The trick with the highest stacks doesn't seem to work any longer.

"*Uhm. Hello, Creator? What else am I missing?*"

"*Your third lesson is individuality. It would serve you to become individually cooperative and cooperatively an individual. It is not because you are all working together that you have to lose your individuality. You are all equal, but not the same and yet you are—depends on perspective. Let the other players play their chips first and place your chips in between the highest stacks."*

Like clockwork, the winning streak starts again, and as soon as the first losing round comes around, Elliott knows better and links up immediately.

"*Is there another lesson?*"

Creator replies, "*We are going to finish this class with your first lesson: trust. Instead of playing five chips on five numbers, you are going to play five chips on one number.*"

"*Which number?*"

"*Number eighteen.*"

Lo and behold, number eighteen is the next winning number.

"*From now on, Elliott, you're on your own. Enjoy!*"

When Elliott finally cashes out with the cashier, he receives $157.50

Elliott is quite happy with the modest gain in monetary funds. His overanalyzing mind is already calculating how much profit he gained that night. "*One hundred fifty seven dollars and fifty cents minus seven dollars and fifty cents, which I lost at the slot machines, is one hundred and fifty dollars. I spent sixty dollars to get the roulette chips so when I subtract sixty dollars from one hundred and fifty dollars, I get?*"

"*Exactly ninety dollars,*" *says Creator smilingly.*

Elliott almost walks into the wall as he comes to that realization: "*My God, that's how this whole trip started. What is the meaning of the number ninety?*"

The minute this new revelation sinks in, Elliott starts sobbing while walking to the car. He must be the only one who walks out of a casino crying when having won money.

"*I will never doubt You again.*"

"*Yes, you will.*"

"*Oh, come on (sob). I'm serious. I will never doubt You again.*"

"*If you say so. But I say you will.*"

THE KEEPER'S MANIFESTO

HARMONIC UNIVERSE 4. 3.8 Million Years AD. Planet Alcyone.

Commander Jane Darkon is reading in the Falcon's relaxation lounge. Its luminescent walls seem to be alive as its colors respond in pattern, texture, and brightness to the ambient tunes that are playing Tom Jobim's Brazilian Bossa Nova tunes, selected from her last trip to Earth. The holographic text projected from the transmitters in her lounge chair is floating right in front.

The Keeper's Manifesto:

First, there are the four universal truths. These are "always" true no matter when or where the question is asked, whether it is in the physical space, subspace, pre-liquid space, or nonphysical realm. From the perspective of absolute infinity, the interpretation of these guidelines may differ, however.

> You and I exist. We exist. We exist together as One.
>
> The One is All, we are All, we are One. The One is more than the sum of its components.
>
> We receive what we put out. Our reality experience is a reflection of who we truly are at any given scale; the Universe is fractal in nature. What happens on a small scale happens on a larger scale and vice versa; they can both influence one another.
>
> Change is constant, except for the four universal truths.

Guidelines of the Elders of the Twelve Tribes

Do unto others—out of love—what you want others to do unto you (or what they want done unto themselves, or what they need), but don't expect the same in return.

Judge not, lest you be judged, because in the judging you are actually identifying an unhealed aspect of yourself. If you are in a position where you are being asked to judge on behalf of two parties, use discernment and view the perspective from both sides carefully; then try and see the bigger picture and the picture around it and so on. How will the judgment affect the Whole, and at what ratios will you apply the energies of mercy versus judgment?

Every person deserves equal opportunity, and the freedom to pursue self-discovery, self-expression, and self-gratification in service to oneselves. In human terms this is known as liberty, equality, brotherhood/sisterhood, and justice for all.

Respect all, and live in joy, gratitude, appreciation. There's nothing that needs to be fixed or that is broken, unless you deem it so; don't let others tell you what to do and think. Everything and every moment is perfect because it is as it should be; happiness comes from accepting what is, not from thinking what it should be. We can change ourselves and how we react to situations, which becomes easier as we know, accept, and love ourselves. Love the other as you love yourself, and, if you don't love yourself (enough), love the other like the One loves each of us unconditionally.

Captain Kyrasha walks up to Commander Jane Darkon.

"Reading up on philosophy or politics?"

"Captain Kyrasha, thanks for joining me. I'd say a bit of both."

"Jane, do you remember when you taught the manifesto you are reading to the new cadets? I remember you saying that the key to those texts is to feel it with your entire being. You were right at so many levels. And that it was a gift from the Lemurians to the humans and, as a consequence, to many other extraterrestrial life-forms. This is an ancient document, Jane, and it is revered across the Universe. If only all of us would appreciate that message a bit faster."

"We would be out of a job, Captain!"

Kyrasha laughs heartily. "Once these galactic wars are over, I wouldn't mind taking a stroll across a few planets and nebulae. Get a break from it all. Nourish myself a bit. But I volunteered out of love for the One to assist in these conflicts, and we all know that the end is always the same, balance and harmony. That is why we are here, so these conflicts end sooner and sooner and every one of us gets to live a life of comfort, ease, and abundant love, instead of pain and suffering."

"There are those who would say you are picking sides, Kyrasha. Aren't we fighting the Geeray after all?"

"You are still amnesiac, Jane. We are caring for both. Each life-form has the right to exist or chose to go extinct. We assist them both in what they really want. However, when one dominant species is meddling in the free will of others, even when the dominated species is experiencing so-called free will, then we volunteer to step in to protect the right of every individual. While the perpetrators have the right to express themselves by enslaving an entire planet of let's say humans, the humans have the right to understand who they truly are and who their enslavers are and then make their free will choice as a society based on truer information versus what they have been fed for thousands of years. After that, they can create their own realities as they see fit. It serves us to educate them while they are slowly waking up. Unfortunately, most of our messengers get killed or ridiculed because it sounds too good to be true. That is why you and your team were sent down. It's a shame you were treated like that by your so-called adversaries and the ones you were trying to save. Their minds are creating their reality. Well, you've experienced it firsthand by volunteering to incarnate there through the veil of forgetfulness, and now you are here waiting to be transferred into a virtual reality to recover from the wounds on your psyche."

"When do you think I can start that healing procedure?" asks Jane.

"About that, yes, we will be docking at the Crystal City in one hour. Your family will be waiting for you, and they have been warned about your condition. They will transfer with you to the Artificial Simulation Recovery Center. For your own protection, we are keeping your consciousness quarantined and under control, in case you weren't aware of it. I'm sorry that it has to be this way, Jane."

"That's OK, Captain, I understand. I just feel like a four-year-old toddler among all you superminds."

"Do I need to remind you how respected you are? There is nothing to be ashamed of. Instead, we all care for you, and we want the best for you. In the meantime, tell me a story about your earthly experience."

"OK, well, one year after my awakening, I had learned many names for Prime Creator: Source, All-That-Is, Universal Energy, God, Supreme Being, Wise One, Ultimate Love, and Pigeon. I also came to realize that there are many higher evolved beings out there that are trying to communicate as a way to assist, while others try to disseminate misinformation. The misinformation is usually done under the guise of a so-called loving guide with a slight distortion in the Sacred Law of One. Some teach indifference and irresponsibility, which do and do not apply according to circumstances and where the Soul is in its development. 'Proceed with caution' is what I learned. Anyway, there are so many entities out there, and since it is hard to figure out who is really who and what they represent, I decided at a certain moment to only communicate with Creator. All the other in-betweeners like deities, fairies, angels, extraterrestrials, etc. I cut off for my own sanity. At least until I got my wits back. So one night, Creator swings by and starts teaching. He is such a patient loving teacher. I always feel awesome in His/Her/Its presence. I am madly in love with Creator."

"I think I know what you are talking about. Once you feel that connection, it is hard to say no to something so amazing," replies Captain Kyrasha.

"So here is what Creator told me, and since you know better than I, you can probably interject your version of reality or not. I'll call it Creator explains the Universe:

"'*First, consider that there is only One-Soul, the All-That-Is, The Unknown Soul. From this perspective imagine that the One-Soul is electricity. It powers all Universes, and every Universe is a different aspect of the One-Soul. For example, a radio, a television, and a light bulb are three different aspects in which electricity can express itself: the radio produces sound, the television produces sound and moving images, and the light bulb produces light. In reality, the One-Soul is that which suffuses and permeates all Universes, all matter, non-matter, antimatter, light, sound, and all other forces, anti-forces and non-forces. Imagine that you live in a television Universe where the element of time exists and you live for a very long time. In that case, you will experience the black-and-white television set evolve to a color television set to a plasma TV, to LCD, to LED TV, and then to matter-less plasma projectors to liquid light TV sets, and then back to its core components, that which the One-Soul is at a basic level, and then so on. What is going on at a cosmic level is the conversion of matter to less-dense matter to no-more-matter to love. At the same time, the love is moving down and cooling down to become matter for the sole purpose of experiencing itself and recreating itself in a more evolved manner. This is what Hermes meant with his statement 'As above, so below. As below, so above.' The Universe is fractal in nature, so what you experience at one level, you will encounter at another level. For example, you performed an exorcism last night with one of your friends, and later that night you see on the news that one guy was abusing his girlfriend and threw her out of her house. Same scenario, where the guy is the invading spirit who threw the original spirit out of her house. Then the police came and detained him. The police was the intervention from the higher realms through you as a vessel. Same intentions, experienced at a different level in a slightly different setting. Another example, when the eel-like alien symbiote was pulled out of your body, you noticed that the evening news described the beaching of an ore fish, which usually only swims in deep water. Again, what happened to you on a small scale, the eel extraction, another part of you experienced also that day on another level, the eel-like ore fish dying on the beach. The principle of Hermes as described above is generally true, but not always. In a system that is rendering itself unstable, the flow of energy from the Unified Field becomes unstable, and, if left unchecked, it will cease to flow and as such, that system will cease to exist in perceived material form. These fail-safe devices have been put in place to protect the whole system. From the timeline whence you came, Earth was destroyed and you were abducted by extraterrestrials whose intent was to sell you to a Soul-farming facility for the harvesting of energy. You were saved by the Arcturians when they beamed you up from the so-called surface of the planet. You were not in California. Instead, you were already on board the Geeray spaceship perceiving to live in your normal environment as part of a hologram, which, as you noted correctly, was severely inadequate in projecting the holographic Universe that I created. The Arcturians came to your rescue and got you off their ship, and after a brief sojourn on their lightships, you were downloaded in a hologram where Earth still exists.'"*

"That is an amazing explanation. The Arcturians saved you, huh?" Kyrasha said smilingly.

"Are you implying it was you that saved me?"

"It depends on how you look at it. Did they rescue you from the surface of the 'planet'? Yes. Unfortunately, the *Falcon* was destroyed, and many Arcturian bodies died. No worries, they are so evolved that they can reconstruct their bodies anywhere any time after disembodiment. You will meet them again. We, the Pleiadians, work very closely with them. We are united through the Intergalactic Federation. We are going to need to get you up to speed on intergalactic politics. It's quite a story, I tell you."

"But Creator told me that story months ago? How can you be the ones that saved me now?"

"Time doesn't exist, Jane, and linear time is the biggest illusion of all. If humans knew how many times they die in a given lifetime and how many times we reconstruct their bodies, they would be much more open to contacting us instead of us having to do it on the sly with memory wipes and holographic inserts. It would make our job easier for sure."

"But what about the Geeray?"

"It is true that a minority of extraterrestrials do not have the best interest at heart for humanity. Unfortunately, they have been controlling the human minds in most timelines up until the Grand Awakening. It is Prime Creator's wish, and as such, it is inevitable. How long it takes to get to the human Paradise and how pleasant the ride is, depends on time and humanity's conscious decision as a collective to want to evolve into the Super Beings that they are. Humans, in fact, are more powerful than the ones that are enslaving them, largely due to their direct connection to the One-Soul. This has created envy from less-evolved extraterrestrials, and they decided to go back in time to enslave humanity's mind. It's a real power trip for them to be able to subdue Divine Beings and make them do anything they want in a so-called voluntary manner. Mostly, this is done through holographic inserts and meddling with the energy bodies that control the mental and the emotional mind so that the individual not so 'freely' chooses to go down the path of separate from the other versus seeing the unity and connectedness in all. They freely give up their own Divine Power and adopt a wanting-to-be-saved or taking-what-I-can attitude, not knowing that they have all the power to create whatever they want for themselves and/or in service to the other. If only they would put their own minds together and set a single clear intent, their reality experience would change fast from having to struggle or fight one another to instant manifestation of matter out of nowhere and having the time and joy to create or do anything they want. Do what you want to do when you want to do it. Who wouldn't want that?"

"You do have a good point there. So what about us?"

"We do it because we love it. And we are helping out of love for our Creator, for ourselves, and for our other selves."

SOURCE EXPLAINS THE NATURE OF GOD AND THE UNIVERSE

HARMONIC UNIVERSE ONE. Twenty-First Century. Planet Earth.

It is late at night, and Elliott wakes up knowing he is in the focused presence of All-That-Is.

"*Do you want to learn more, my dear Elliott?*"

"*Yes, please, I love you, Father. Of course! Thank you so much for patiently teaching me. And I'm sorry for being a petulant rebelling teenager once in a while.*"

"*That's OK. I created you to behave this way. For now, I am teaching you so that you can disseminate this knowledge to your brothers and sisters across the whole planet. So let's start with the beginning of the Universe.*"

"*You mean the Big Bang?*"

Source chuckles. "*No, way before that.*" And then He/She continues, "*In the beginning, there was nothing, and the Supreme Being wanted to explore. So He moved IT's singularity, Her consciousness. The amount used at the first movement was infinitely small, because I did not want to lose Myself. After the first move, you could say there were two dots next to one another. For the purpose of teaching, let's use a visually appealing distance, let's say two inches. As I could safely move to the right, I figured I could safely move to the left, the opposite direction.*

"*Imagine these were only small dots next to one another.*

"*I knew I could move safely in one plane of existence, and I decided to add a second plane by correct assumption that above and below Me was room for one dot each. This had to be perpendicular relative to the first movement, because otherwise, the dots would be intersected beyond the one-point connectedness. The Celtic Cross was born right there.*

"Eventually, I figured that I would also add one more dimension: forward and backward.

"The addition of the third dimension creates a perceived asymmetry, known as the negative and the positive, or the male and the female, or the light and the dark, or could also randomly have been annotated the yellow and the blue, because from my perspective there is no value judgment on either. Use your favorite terminology per your own mutual agreements. It is when you see both as One that true understanding arises, and you begin to merge or unite your perspectives.

"After adding the forward and the backward dots, I then had seven connected dots or spheres. Dots and spheres can be considered interchangeable words in this narrative. Then I added more dots, and lines came into appearance.

"Without the presence of gravity or other subspace distortions, which were completely absent at that point in time, light moves in a linear fashion. In your reality, straight lines are associated with the Masculine and curved lines are associated with the Feminine—purely by convention and mutual agreement. I ponder whether this is because a certain percentage of male sexual organs appear in a straight line when erect, and female appearances seem curvier. It doesn't matter here, because both were created at the same time. It just depends on your perspective. The singular dot when magnified becomes a sphere or, when the dot and the sphere are combined to highlight the fractal nature of the Universe, it becomes the All-Seeing-Eye.

"At any given location on the sphere, you can move to the next point in a straight line. They were co-created and they co-inside. Written differently, "co-inside" becomes "coin side," meaning there are two sides to each coin. In this way, you can look at the Creation of God from the inside out or from the outside in or both. I will end the lesson here. That is a lot of information to absorb for a young one."

THE CURIOSITY OF BRUCE

HARMONIC UNIVERSE ONE. Twenty-First Century. Planet Earth.

One of Elliott's closest friends is swinging by to catch up on life. While enjoying the violet-hued clouds from the balcony, Bruce confronts Elliott about his newfound interests in spirituality, energy healing, and channeling.

"So what is up with you, Elliott? You've been acting out of character for quite a few months and then these crazy visions you keep having. What's the newest and latest?"

"Well, it's true that things are changing with me, for the better I think. I'm meditating every day now."

"You know how to sit in proper meditation pose?"

"I don't believe much in following strict rules. For meditation I prefer to lie down. Others can sit in lotus position, or in a chair, or lie down on the ground or in bed. It doesn't really matter as I long as I make the time to go inside at least once a day, preferably more."

"So what do you do in your meditations? And what do you get out of it?"

"Well, first I create sacred space. You want to hear my latest prayer or incantation to create sacred space?"

"Sure," Bruce says, chuckling.

"Don't laugh. Here goes: 'I call on all my guides, my master guides, my guardian angels, and my God-given extraterrestrial beings who have only my highest and greatest good at heart, and I ask to be completely surrounded by the blue flame, and the gold flame, and I ask to be completely surrounded and immersed by Holy Love and Holy Light and I ask that anything that is here or that wishes to approach that is not pure love be instantly transmuted into love by this light. Now I ask for help with my intention, which is to experience unconditional love through connecting fully with the I am that I am, I am. And I thank you for doing this. Amen."

"Wow, that's a lot of words, but it sounds good. You're calling on ETs?"

"Yes, but only the ones that have our best interest at heart."

"You seriously believe in ETs?"

"Dude, this galaxy has a hundred billion times a hundred billion stars. I think it is rather arrogant to believe that we are the only ones around."

"I'll give you that. Sure. But how would they come here and why?"

"Bruce, you're thinking naively arrogant. The signpost for a primitive society is that society believe themselves to be evolved, when they clearly are not. Look at the depictions of the Mayan and the Egyptian Gods. They were highly evolved beings who came here. There is plenty of evidence that they have been and still are around. The Egyptian pyramids, the excavation of superlarge humans, and elongated skulls. You just need to open your eyes. I have worked with quite a few of them, to be honest. According to the Elohim, whom people in the Old Testament refer to as angels, humanity and planet Earth is an experiment to store information in the form of genetic codes, a grandiose idea that requires the largest diversity to store vast amounts of data. At the same time, our human, plant, and animal vehicles can be used to progress Souls after they decide to separate from Creator. The miracle of the human experience was that in one lifetime, supposedly, a human Being/Soul could transmute from physical to nonphysical without going through the death process and then return to Creator while maintaining its individual identity. We are on track to reclaim that ability."

"Now you are going way overboard, Elliott. You lost me there. Why can't we go from physical to nonphysical now, and why then does everybody die? The only sure thing, up until now apparently, was death and taxes."

"Our DNA has been tampered with, and a lot of it has been rendered useless. This is the junk DNA that our molecular biologists are talking about. Also, we have twelve strands of DNA, not two strands of DNA."

Bruce replies chokingly, "Seriously, this coming from a molecular biologist such as yourself? Even I know that we have two strands of DNA, and that's it. Watson and Crick discovered it in 1952."

Elliott remains unfazed: "You have two physical strands, and ten other strands, which you will never encounter fully in physical reality. Some people have even more strands. It is part of the diversity experiment."

Bruce is still not convinced: "That's a cop-out."

And Elliott replies, "I did not believe it either when Creator was teaching, but last month I noticed an article in *Scientific American* highlighting the birth of a baby with three strands of DNA, which up until then was scientifically impossible. That, and during meditation, I've actually left my body and seen my DNA on the other side. It is quite beautiful."

"I'll stay in the middle on this one. Why would aliens meddle with our DNA?"

"For them it was a matter of survival of their species. As a consequence, we were turned into a slave race. Originally, our females could chose when to get pregnant. Now, they are genetically forced to ovulate every month and breed as much as they can to generate happy obedient slaves. Have you ever wondered why the world population has increased so dramatically?"

"Are you saying that we are enslaved?"

"Yes, that's a good way of looking at it. The best prison is one where you do not realize that you are in prison."

"I think most people will label you crazy when you say that."

"Well, let's talk about normal. What is normal? Is normal what the majority believes or is normal the original design? If you take the first definition, then I can be labeled crazy. If you take the latter than the majority is crazy believing that this is the way it is supposed to be. Are you happy with the way this world is going?"

"No, but there's nothing I can do about it."

"And that is what they want you to believe. I am not the first one to say this. In fact, there have been many messengers and whistle-blowers, but most have been ridiculed, persecuted, nailed to a cross, or burnt as witches. What will it be this time around? You cannot trust your mind. Plato already knew this. It has been going on for thousands of years. What does your heart tell you?"

Bruce replies meekly, "When I hear the story about our original destiny it feels good, but when I hear the story of our enslavement, it gets me nervous to say the least."

"There is no need to be afraid, Bruce. There's much help behind the scenes. The enlightened evolved beings work through a code of noninterference, which means that help is always offered to those who ask, but they cannot assist on your behalf without you asking, unless it is a matter of life and death. And help is usually offered in ways beyond your comprehension."

"That sounds like the Prime Directive from *Star Trek*."

"Where do you think the scriptwriters of *Star Trek* got it from?"

"All right, I have reached my limits here. Can we go out and have a few drinks and not talk about this for a while?"

"Now we're talking. Let us go to Baja Betty's for margaritas."

ELLIOTT'S DIARY: THE PROCESS IN PROSE

HARMONIC UNIVERSE ONE. Twenty-First Century. Planet Earth.
And from the harvest, the wheat is separated from the chaff.
Fear not, the Goddess has a big bosom.
She loves plenty, forgives easily,
And wishes nothing but the best for all;
However one defines "it."
Who will you serve?
Let the White Paladin be your guide,
And follow his equine roots to sea,
And flow with the current of rebirth and fortitude.
Let Chariots of Fire, like a Phoenix,
Burst from the naval ire,
And purge all that binds us;
Keep us on our true path.
Go with Dante, cut yourself down,
And lie broken, in pieces,
Because the pieces can survive the sieve of Thor,
While thorns are put asunder.
Then follow the Rainbow Bridge to the land of Sun and Honey.
Stop. Think. Feel. Be. Have. Relax. Love.
Linger once more in the rays of the Sun.
Because when all rays are one,
The Son is suddenly Sun,
And the quest starts beyond what is binding.

THE DOUBLE-HEADED COBRA

HARMONIC UNIVERSE ONE. Twenty-First Century. Planet Earth.

During one of his many meditations, Elliott receives a vision about two cobras facing one another and they are looking at each other through a window. They are mimicking and anticipating the moves of the other's head and seemingly striving to stay in balance. The two cobras are, weirdly so, connected through the same body. As such, the first cobra's tail ends up in the body of the second cobra.

While still inside his head, Elliott speaks, "*Creator, what does this image mean?*"

"*The two cobras represent power and knowledge of the unknown. At the same time, it was also sent to teach that while most people are afraid when they encounter a cobra, a cobra is not afraid of a cobra, because it realizes they are family. They are the same. An ant is terribly afraid when it would perceive a human, but a human doesn't freak out when it sees another human, unless they are at war. That is why the single body was sent. It would serve humanity to realize that they are all part of One Body and what they see through the window of their eyes, which is an analogy for their perception of the virtual reality they live in, is basically themselves reflected in a mirror. And since the separation is falsely real in physical, it serves to cooperate with one another rather than antagonize one another. Imagine that one cobra head becomes aggressive and strikes the other cobra head. Both of them would hurt, because the nerves connected in the body will transfer that pain to the striking head as well. Now some people react out of pain and hurt and lash out, which is also the option for cobra number two. But when the second cobra knows what is going on, it might change its reaction and try to understand why the first cobra attacked and what it needs in order to prevent further attacks. Or it might send a warning to the other cobra like 'Hey, here is what is going on. I am trying to help you. But if you do not stop attacking me, I will have to defend myself and then, over time, we will hurt more and more and possibly we will both die. Because we are the same body, just saying. Why don't we try to get along? What do you need to feel safe, secure, and how do you want to explore and express yourself in an atmosphere of mutual respect and appreciation?'"*

"You make it sound so easy. So what do I do when I get attacked?"

"Highly evolved beings allow the attacker to experience what they want to experience, and so they would let their body die out of love for the other for the simple reason that they can leave their bodies and build a new one elsewhere instantly. Now you are not there yet. There have been humans who achieved this feat, and some of them are described in Paramahansa Yogananda's autobiography, so it is not impossible for you either. If your strongest desire is to survive in your current physical body, then defend yourself, fight back, but with an attitude of love, not with an attitude of revenge. Or you could decide that this ride is no longer worth it and allow the other to end your life. An equally valid option. Once you reemerge from your physical body, you will experience extreme bliss as you return to all that you are. You see, from your Soul's perspective being born into physicality sucks, because 'you' go from all-knowing quasi infinite being into a tiny clumpy mass of cells. That being said, there is mystery and surprise in not knowing, and your finite experience can be considered a wonderful gift as such. In fact, the less you know, the better the experience. The death experience, something that is feared so terribly by your fellow humans, is a very beautiful experience. And once you are 'on the other side,' you get to decide, barring certain hurdles that you will be explained later, what else you want to experience, and you and I will sit together with a whole team and draft another lifetime of experiences here on Earth or any other location in the Universe. Everything is possible. Isn't that amazing? Do you see now that my greatest joy is to give you what you want?"

"I haven't been getting exactly what I want, I gotta tell you that."

"Yes, you have. You are confined to thinking within your Ego mind, and that is very limited. As such, it creates unease and unhappiness as your Ego does not see what you want. The Ego mind is an artificial consciousness that arose after the Earth was placed under quarantine, and it has been the only way with which humans in general have been able to experience their

reality. Trust that all is taken care of and, at the same time, create with your mind, your body, and your spirit the experience that you most desire. Now what do you most desire? Align these priorities with all that you are, which means beyond your Ego mind, and you will be amazed what happens next. Then you truly will see that you always get what you want."

"All right, I'm getting a headache here. Can't you teach me with a physical body instead of talking in my head all the time?"

"You have asked, and so it is given, instantly."

"Really, where is my live flesh-and-blood teacher? I don't see anyone."

Chuckling follows that statement, and Creator continues, "*Patience, young one. The moment when your teacher appears is created the second you ask, so when you understand time a little better, I will remind you of this conversation. But I assure you, your teacher will appear in a manner that I think is most surprising, and I hope you find these jewels of surprise with the mind-set of a child that is amazed and grateful for his or her presents. Everything you asked for, are asking for, and will ask for in this lifetime and others will be given to you. When you get to experience them is partly up to you and largely up to You, which is Me."*

THE TEACHER APPEARS IN FLESH

HARMONIC UNIVERSE ONE. Twenty-First Century. Planet Earth.

A few days after his conversation with Creator, Elliott arrives at his bank to take care of financial matters. After making the beneficial transactions, he notices a person sitting down who is seemingly in need of help.

Elliott approaches the young man.

"Can I help you with anything?"

"I just need to get out of here. I don't know where I am. This is not where I'm supposed to be."

Elliott continues caringly.

"OK, are you hungry? You want to grab some lunch? What's your name?"

"Yes, that would actually be nice. My name is Kaleb."

They walk across the street to the local diner and are seated within a few minutes. The young blond-haired twenty-something-year-old then starts loudly proclaiming a tirade of Bible scripture texts and the like.

"I am the alpha and the omega archangel. I was sent here by Jehovah. The Most High. All these people around us, they have no clue. And they will perish in the fire." And the loud uttering of biblical verses keeps going on and on.

To no avail, Elliott is trying to get a word in to calm him down. Eventually, out of embarrassment, he throws a twenty-dollar bill on the table and gets up. "Let's go to my place. I will cook you some food."

They leave immediately, and it becomes clear that Kaleb, still spouting Divine messages, is homeless. The messages are rather erratic, and there is little coherence in his replies.

When they arrive at Elliott's place, he shows Kaleb the bathroom so he can take a shower.

"Here are some fresh clothes. Give me yours when you are done with the shower, and I will wash them. I'll be upstairs cooking food. Feel free to come up when you are ready."

While Elliott is preparing spaghetti, he links up with Creator.

"Is he really an archangel?"

"Yes. You asked for a teacher in the flesh. Didn't you?"

"But he is homeless, and he sounds crazy."

"You are judging too fast. There is much wisdom to his words. Listen carefully and with an open heart."

"What is he going to teach?"

"What you need to know now."

"I don't like it when you talk in mysteries."

"All life is a mystery. Enjoy your time with him. Good luck!"

So Elliott decides to call his new friend Miley who is an angel expert according to her own words.

"Miley, I have an archangel in the flesh here. I feel out of my league. Can you come over here?"

"An archangel? Yes, of course. I will be right over."

He also texts his other friend, Rory, who self-proclaims that he knows way more than what is really going on. And who claims that he is older than Elliott in terms of other worldly knowledge and experience.

"Hey, Rory, I have a guy here at my place who claims to be an archangel. You want to swing by?"

"For real? Or are you just trying to get me over for a drink? What is his color and wingspan?"

"For real, I think. I can't see his wings. He looks normal to me, except he acts crazy."

"Take a picture and send to me."

So Elliott takes a picture after asking if that would be OK and sends it to Rory.

"Oh, wow, he is old and powerful. I am leaving now. I will be at your place in twenty minutes."

Five minutes later, the archangel is ominously smiling, and Elliott receives a new text message from Rory.

"Elliott, I can't open my front door or any of my windows to get out of my apartment. I guess he does not want me to be there. I want to hear all about it tomorrow. Good luck!"

"You still have doubts that I'm an archangel? Let me show you something." And he starts stomping his feet up and down commanding the Earth to be shaken.

"I have called forth an earthquake. Did you feel it?"

"No, actually," says Elliott, and he goes pensive. "*Maybe this guy is just a fraud after all. Maybe it is all a fraud, and I am going crazy. Why did I even believe in all this nonsense?*"

Meantime, Miley has arrived at Elliott's front door of the apartment building, and Elliott has to take the elevator down to open the door. While the doors of the elevator are closing, his neighbor Tim asks him to hold the elevator, and he shouts excitedly, "Did you feel the earthquake?"

"When?"

"A few minutes ago. A 6.3 on the Richter scale. I just looked it up. Cool huh?"

"Yeah. Way cool," Elliott replies, and in his mind he thinks, "*Oh my God, this is really happening.*"

He opens the door to Miley, and when they are back in the unit, his roommate, Eman, is sitting across from Kaleb, signaling with his eyes that he thinks this guy is out of his mind. Miley starts talking to the archangel, and he calms down during the course of their conversation.

"He's definitely got angelic knowledge," says Miley.

"Let me prove once more that I, the alpha and the omega, command the heavens and the earth, and all the archangels. I command Archangel Gabriel to come down and be with us."

Nothing much seems to happen, and suddenly Miley starts sobbing uncontrollably. Elliott brings his face to Eman's ear and whispers, "I did not invite her to make a scene here. Sorry, dude. I wish she could get a grip on herself."

Right after he finishes that sentence, he feels streams of energy entering his body, and Elliott himself starts sobbing uncontrollably, mouthing to Eman, "I'm sorry, I can't help it."

"This is too weird," says Eman, and he leaves the apartment.

Miley and Elliott continue their wonderful cry. It is the most exquisite sadness that they have ever experienced, and when it is finally over, they wish they could experience it again.

"Now that your roommate is gone, I can actually start teaching," says Kaleb in a calm and this time normal voice and intonation.

"Elliott, I came here today to let you know that things are not as they seem. You have grown a lot in the last months, and you have accumulated much light and consciousness to the extent that you are drawing attention to yourself, which means we only have a small window of opportunity before the other side decides to recruit you."

"The other side? What other side?"

"Elliott, there is a war going on at a galactic scale. Let's call it angels versus demons. You have heard about them in many ancient and sacred texts, and I am here to tell you that it is really going on. I am also here to tell you that you are of angelic descent, and you are a humanized reincarnated angel, just like Miley."

Elliott is shocked. "Miley, is this true?"

Firmly she answers, "Yes, it is."

Flabbergasted Elliott yells, "Why didn't you tell me all this before?"

And Miley calmly replies, "Because you would not have believed me, and you would have run away."

Elliott's voice shakes as he is trying to absorb this information. "That's true. I'm still trying to wrap my head around all of this. It is a lot to assimilate. I am an angel?"

"Yes, you are part of the Elohim, a galactic entity of light. Why do you think it is so easy for you to communicate with Creator?"

"I need to get some air. I have to go outside."

"I would prefer that you stay here for a little while longer. There is much more I need to tell you."

"Make me!" Elliott spits out. He gets up and walks to the balcony door. He gets about half way to the exit when he feels an invisible force pushing him backward until he is seated back into the ruby red chair.

"Now that I have your attention, can we continue?" says the archangel softly.

Indignantly, Elliott says, "OK. You got me on that one. That is impressive. But why me? And what does it matter?"

And Kaleb remains surprisingly calm in his words. "Why not you? The choices you make are important. You have a lot of skills, but with great power comes responsibility. Or not—that is your choice. You can also choose the other side if you want."

Elliott blurts out, "Why would I choose for demons?"

And a soft but stern reply follows from the archangel. "It's not all black and white, you know. Different perspectives. We believe that all life needs to be honored and that we are all equal, no matter which skill set or DNA, because we are all one. The other side believes that a select few should rule the masses and take advantage of them because they do not know what is best for them."

Elliott is overwhelmed, and a few tears roll down his cheeks, when he asks meekly. "Do I have to choose? Now? And what will happen?"

"You do not have to choose, in which case you will remain as you are, but your life will be miserable as the other side will cut you down every way they can, and your Soul will cry out because it will be forced by your choice to live a life unlived. You also do not have to choose now. When you do, you will go through a fast transformation, and you will also get your wings."

Elliott looks straight into Kaleb's eyes and spits out, "I don't see your wings, just saying."

Chuckling, the archangel replies, "The wings are in the ethereal dimensions. They are not used to fly. That is a common misconception, but they do serve a purpose. They can be used to generate and guide ultrahigh frequencies into patterns that are beneficial for the physical, emotional, mental, and spiritual bodies of the people around you, especially when you put your single-minded focus on healing."

And the archangel continues, "Now, Elliott, please take a pen and paper and write this down. First, you need to clear away all the clutter. Imagine that you are a computer. Every time you say something or think something, the Universe listens and reads the command line that you spoke, thought, or wrote. Some wishes or utterances or intentions or goals that you proclaimed have not come to fruition yet, and according to Prime Creator all wishes have to be fulfilled. So the Universe is working through a long list of all the things you have said in your life from the minute you were born. Do you even remember what you asked for when you were six or in other lives? Some of those wishes are coming through now or later in your life. If your sole intent is to go through this transformation, you have to cancel and rescind all prior requests. You are cleaning the slate, as a matter of speaking. It is like having a blackboard filled with clutter, and you are wiping the clutter away with a sponge so the Universe can focus on what you really want, which is what you need to restate after you have cleared your intentions. So when you are ready, now or later, read out loud the following sentences: I rescind all unfinished intentions, wishes, wants, and desires, except the One Intention that I set forth here as 'state your primary intent.' From now on, any intentions, wants, and desires can only be set through the ceremony invoking the Creator of All-That-Is. All other input received and output transmitted are secondary to the creation of my physical experience. The One Intention is my only and my primary intention, so help me God, so be it, it is done."

Elliot sighs wearily. "OK, I wrote that down. What else?"

Kaleb smiles, sensing his unease with these protocols or guidelines that are being handed down to him; Elliott does have issues with submitting to outside authorities.

"There is indeed more, young one," Kaleb speaks slowly. "Write down the following, which you can use as many times as you want. Especially when you feel tired or not feeling like the real you.

"I call back all the energy that I spent outside of me, and I put it back inside me with love and healing, and all the energy within and around me that is not mine, I release to the Universe with love and healing. Thank you, Universe. Amen.

"You want to continue, Elliott?"

"Yes, it doesn't look like I have a choice anyway, right?"

"You do have a choice, but not in the way that you think. OK, next, you have a lot of cords of attachment emanating from you. You need to cut those or ask Archangel Michael to cut them for you, or Creator."

Elliott's face lights up. "Archangel Michael is a good one. I have talked to him on many occasions. What are cords of attachment?"

Patiently Kaleb explains, "They are hollow energetic tubes that link you to other individuals or entities, and they drain energy from you. They do not serve you at all. Asking for these to be cut does not cut the love cord, so it does not negatively affect relationships with other people from a love aspect."

Elliott is still not fully on board with all the mumbo jumbo. "Is this for real? Come on, really?"

"Elliott, it is more real than you think. These cords are a lot tougher to cut than you can imagine. There, as well as here, those cords can regrow or reattach, especially when dark forces are in play. I will remind you to watch the movie *The Matrix* again, so you can envision these attachment cords better when you are doing these meditations."

The archangel continues teaching and does not seem to get tired at all. Elliott, on the other hand, has to call it a night when it is 4:44 a.m. Time to go to bed for another day of real-life science fiction.

THE ARTIFICIAL RECOVERY CYBORG

HARMONIC UNIVERSE 4. 3.8 Million Years AD. Planet Wakala.

The office of Dr. Brobol is located at Planet Wakala, a water planet in the Andromeda system. Many advanced species reside here for relaxation and experience. It is ideally suited for brainiacs, almost like Silicon Valley in California. Commander Jane Darkon is guided into the waiting room. The friendly staff member greets Jane in the friendliest way possible.

"Good morning, Jane Darkon. Welcome to Dr. Brobol's office. He will be right with you."

Jane replies amicably, "Thank you, dear. I brought my sister Kayla with me to monitor the whole process."

Five minutes later, Dr. Brobol enters the room and addresses Jane with a big smile on his face. "Commander Darkon, welcome. A pleasure to see you in flesh, so to speak."

"No need for formalities, Doctor. When do we get started?"

"Have you read the files we sent to you, and do you agree with the treatment?"

"Yes, I do, Doctor. One question, though. You are going to download my consciousness into an Artificial Recovery Cyborg (ARC), whose name is Dr. Elliott Himmerept. I will walk in during a so-called crisis moment of the drone, and I will adopt all his memories and forget all my current memories. That young male drone will then relive part of the traumas that I went through but to a less severe degree than I experienced, and mostly in the dream state, so that eventually all trauma is released. Is that correct?"

"Indeed, it is."

"Couldn't I stay female in gender?"

"You could, but for your process it is more optimal to choose a male counterpart to minimize any relationships with your former life."

"I am a bit nervous. Are you sure this is the best option?"

"I understand that you are nervous, but there is no risk and you will be taken care of from here. There is nothing that can go wrong at any time. Even if you would accidentally die, we are able to create a duplicate from the original from the last backup, and then the memory is altered. Backups are taken multiple times daily when the drone is resting or sleeping or in meditation."

"What happens to me when the drone sleeps?"

"Your conscience is able to leave the body and join with the real You, the Higher Self. The Ego mind, which we have to program in artificially to mimic the circumstances on Earth, ceases to exist separately during sleep and merges with your unconscious and higher mind during which time healing takes place by exchange of information."

"So what is the next step?"

"We will walk you to the lab, and you will lie down in a bio-stasis tube, where your body will be kept. We will extract your mental, emotional, and spiritual bodies from the physical body, map the energy patterns in our mainframe, reconfigure them in mathematical equations, and download these equations into the drone. Its DNA is designed to accept these equations, and you will wake up continuing in the life of the drone. Do you want to take a look at your future drone-self?"

"Sure."

"Computer, display on a three-dimensional spatial grid versus time the Dr. Elliott Himmerept files. Set timeline destination for May through June 2012."

Computer voice: "Timeline settings established. Starting video."

A holographic blue-white display lights up above Dr. Brobol's crystalline desk.

Jane and the doctor can hear Elliott's voice. "What is going on? What is this beam in my head? What do these images mean?"

Dr. Brobol says to Commander Darkon, "This is where the download of the necessary information for your recovery happened."

"I feel like I'm looking into a dollhouse. So how do you plan on taking care of me while I am down there?" asks Jane Darkon.

They can see Elliott walking to the medicine cabinet for his sleeping pills.

"This is how we can intervene. Computer, please relay my voice so the drone can hear me."

Dr. Brobol speaks through a light cable floating in front of his mouth, and both Kayla and Jane can hear his voice echo in Elliott's bedroom.

"This process will take a few hours. Please don't take the sleeping pill. Relax. You will be fully energized in the morning."

They see Elliott's puzzled look and how he meekly gets back to bed and lies down to undergo the information download procedure.

"We have a couple of hours for the download to complete. In the meantime, we need to get you prepped. Would you follow me to the lab, please?"

ALIENS VERSUS ANGELS

HARMONIC UNIVERSE ONE. Twenty-First Century. Planet Earth.

After his encounter with the archangel, Elliott wants to learn more and decides to go to a class at the local metaphysical bookstore, which is themed "the history of magic and mysticism."

He arrives a bit early, and he gets seated and starts scanning the other participants briefly. When he looks at a cross-legged young lady dressed in a short, green skirt, his eyes wander over her legs, and he can see her bone radiating white light.

"*Is that light coming from her bones, or is it just a reflection of the light in the room?*" He looks around, but the door is closed and only two candles are burning, which puts a warm atmosphere in the room.

"*Come on, Elliott, do not freak out. You are probably just imagining this.*" He wipes his eyes, but the light-emitting bones in her legs remain lit up. Her long blonde-haired friend, dressed in pale blue jeans, smiles at him and lifts her jeans a bit so he can see a portion of her ankles and lower legs, and they are light-giving bone structures too.

"*This is weird!*" Elliott thinks and then focuses on the teacher, who starts explaining the course. During the course they are invited to think about a goal that they want to achieve. And the teacher asks them to write down the first thought that comes in mind without thinking too much.

Elliott writes down, "To meet and connect."

Next she asks the class to envision an image that comes with the goal. Elliott sees a light spiral in his mind, and he starts drawing it out. One by one, each of the students explains what they wrote on their paper. When it is Elliott's turn, he shows the drawing to the audience, and the two white-light-legged ladies gasp in a mixture of surprise and elation.

When the class is over, the young lady with the white light legs comes over to Elliott and asks, "Who are you?"

"Funny, I was going to ask you the same question. Your legs are not lit up anymore. Batteries ran out of power? I am Elliott, by the way."

"I am Lexie, and my friend here is Dani. That question about our legs is not important right now. I have to show you something."

She whips out her phone and searches through her pictures. "I have been drawing these for weeks. I just could not stop drawing them." And she shows him pictures of her paintings, all light spirals.

"Why did you draw that spiral?" she asks Elliott.

"I see it in my mind, Lexie. I got quite some stories about my experiences. I gotta tell you."

"Why don't we go to your place and catch up?"

When they arrive at his place, Elliott tells them about his encounter and interactions with Creator and how he sometimes calls him Pigeon.

"Pigeon! Oh my God. They are going to be laughing about that for a long time. How did you connect to Creator?"

"Well, the first time he just pulled me out of my body, and since then I have tried to get into heaven a few times. I have succeeded, but each time I get the answer that my methods are too hard and to try again. The easiest one so far is a meditation where I set the following intention: I wish to connect with the Universal Energy, the I am that I am, I am. I say that in my head for ten to twenty minutes, and voila, instant heaven. But it does not work all the time. The other one is a meditation where I see myself going through a series of star gates. They look light spheres that enter my head. I fill them up with light, and when they are full, then the sphere or star gate detaches, and I seem to go through a wormhole to the next sphere. The first spheres fill up quickly, but the last spheres take a long time. At sphere thirteen, I usually end up in the white hot room of amazingness."

Excitedly Lexie asks, "Would you mind taking us up there through your meditation?"

And Elliott replies, defeated, "I am not sure if I can do that."

Lexie does not want to give up that easily, though. "Let us try anyway. Nothing wrong with trying. Just merge with us and takes us with you."

And Elliott complies easily after that confidence booster. A few minutes later, Elliott, Lexie, and Dani get comfortable in a chair. They close their eyes, and Elliott focuses on merging their energies and then sets his intent on the thirteen fireball meditation. It takes a lot more effort this time to fill up the thirteen spheres, and he utilizes the power symbols a few times to add more power to the intent; it feels like the energy is turbocharged when he utters these words in his mind. Eventually, they get to the thirteenth level where they meet Creator.

"*Ah, you're back, I see. Good job. And you brought friends? I will talk to them separately if you don't mind.*"

"*Not at all, go ahead.*"

"*I am talking to the three of you separately and at the same time, and I want to tell you, Elliott, that you are doing great. You will be going through a process of purification, a fast purification. I suggest you learn how to clear crystallized thought patterns, which is what your Buddhist describe as karmic imprint clearing. Basically, what you thought before is what you will be experiencing later. If you think it long enough or repeatedly, like a belief, than it will show up in your physical experience quite a lot. Be careful what you think, Elliott. To clear stuck beliefs or other energy patterns, do a meditation and envision a tunnel going up at a ninety-degree angle toward a bright light. Go upward in the tunnel toward the light. Once you merge with the bright light, let it fill your body. This is a visualization that helps you vibrate at a higher level. You will then notice darker spots within yourself. These are the crystallized lower vibrating thought patterns that you want to dissolve. Slow down your consciousness and place your consciousness in these dark spots and let it fill the entirety of the crystallized pattern. It will have a distinct feel and shape, and you may get imprints on what is behind it, but you do not really need to know what it is. Let these imprints move through you. Then imagine white light filling in the space of the thought pattern until it is fully filled. Then call down a bright light sun into the crystallized pattern. This will shatter the whole construct, and the photonic energy created from this process can then be used to rebuild your DNA. Keep doing this for a few other patterns and then go back from the light into the tunnel downward back to where you started. Play with it. You will have fun with it.*"

Elliott goes through the exercise and finally feels himself waking up in his sofa. At the same time, Lexie and Dani are coming by.

"Well, that was a trip," says Lexie. "I ended up with Creator and the first thing He says is, "You are not supposed to be here, and yet so it is supposed to be. He advised me to live a life on Earth because that is why I was born here." Excitedly she tells about her trip, and so does Dani when it is her turn.

"Elliott, you are an energy healer, right? Can I please swing by with my boyfriend tomorrow? He does not believe that we are energy first and matter later. I would love for him to get a feel about it.

"Sure, Lexie, no problem. Bring him by."

The day after, Lexie brings her boyfriend, Sven, over to Elliott's place. Elliott starts the usual healing experience, and while he is at it, he gets the mental suggestion to take a look at Sven's Akashic records. The Akashic records are basically the "hall of records" for everything that has happened, and will potentially happen, to your Soul. He receives a few insights from his guides and cleans up the mess, which Elliott perceives as light energy balls in different sizes and colors. After twenty minutes or so, Sven is all good to go.

Sven is perplexedly at peace. "Oh my God, Elliott, I feel so much better, and I felt energy or whatever it is moving around. That was weird, but I feel good. Surprisingly good. Thanks, dude."

"No problem, Sven. I always say you have to experience an energy healing to believe it. It can't be understood based on logic alone. I'm glad you liked it."

Lexie jumps in, saying, "Can I have a healing too?"

"Sure, Lexie, just lie down and close your eyes."

When Elliott goes into the healing session with Lexie, he also wants to see if anything needs to be addressed in her Akashic records.

"Lexie, I am going to look at your Akashic records. I am closing my eyes now."

Two minutes later, Elliott utters frustrated, "I can't see anything."

Lexie replies, "My records are sealed. Did you ask permission to see them?"

Slightly annoyed, Elliot asks, "No. Do I have your permission to look at them?"

"Yes."

The minute Lexie gives her approval, Elliott notices in his mind two large doors opening, almost like in the movie *Jurassic Park*. That was new to him.

"All right, I'm going in," Elliott says, but nothing much happens, and Elliott is staring into nothingness.

"Lexi, I still can't see anything. I'm sorry."

"I vibrate at a higher level than you. Increase your frequency."

This is costing Elliott focus and energy, and he is about to give up when suddenly he feels something else lifting him. A few seconds later, he sees the orbs, and they both exclaim at the same time, "I *see you*!"

Her boyfriend, who was watching the healing, yells out, "No F——king way?"

Elliott gasps right after, "Who the hell are you?"

"What do you mean?" replies Lexie innocently.

In a stern manner, Elliott replies, "Look, Lexie, I have seen many Akashic records, and yours are only white-colored orbs, all the same size, on one line, and if you look far enough, the orbs form a circle. This is impossible. Who are you?"

"Who do you think I am, Elliott?"

"You are either an alien or an angel, but you are not the average human."

Lexie calmly replies, "Well, maybe angels can be aliens?" She laughs and continues, "Just kidding. I have done a lot of Soul work, and I'm glad it shows."

Next up for a healing is Dani, and the same impeccable Akashic records show up again.

Elliott thinks, "*Her too? Aliens work in pairs? I need to do some more research on Soul work so I can clean up my own records and figure out what Akashic records look like for aliens.*"

When all is said and done, Elliott wants to go back to a normal life soon. "Well, that was fun, ladies, but I really have to go meet my friends. They are celebrating life."

Dani smiles, "Sure, can we drop you off somewhere? And let's plan on meeting up soon. OK?"

"Yes, ladies. That would be awesome. Can you drop me at Moe's? It is a bar nearby."

A few moments later, he meets up with his friends Jeff, Beckster, and Christopher at Moe's. They enjoy a wonderful time together. While

Elliott is on his way to the restroom, Christopher confronts him and becomes the voice of his worst fears.

"Elliott, all your friends are seriously concerned about your mental health. These stories you tell are probably mostly made up and spiced up with your imagination and your need for attention. Are you sure you want to do this to yourself? Quite a lot of our common friends do not want to socialize with you anymore, and I am not sure how much longer the rest are going to take it."

If Elliott would have been completely sober, he could have elevated himself out of the situation, and he would have thanked Christopher for showing a side of him that he yet has to make peace with. Christopher does not realize the impact of his words, and they were meant out of genuine concern. The part of Elliott that he was unknowingly showing to him was doubt. Even after all these experiences, Elliott is still afraid that this is not real and that he is imagining it. The message is sometimes too big to bear, and he wonders why is this happening to him. Elliott is visibly dazed, off balance, and going into a downward spiral. In front of his closed eyelids, he is also reliving a past life at the end of which he basically hanged himself. Reliving that in his mind also compels him to saying good-bye to his current life. Elliott breaks downs and starts sobbing heavily. Christopher is seriously concerned and offers to drive him home. When they arrive at his residence, Christopher voices that concern.

"Do not do anything crazy tonight, Elliott. You are a mess."

"Well, if you worry about dying, don't. Dying is easy because you reemerge as the Infinite Being that you truly are. Getting born sucks, Christopher, because your consciousness is compressed in this tiny glob of clay, and you have to relive the illusion of being finite and separate. In absolute reality, we all are Divine Beings and we are all One living in Unity, yet individuated until we merge with All-That Is."

"Elliott, is killing yourself following the path?"

"Fuck this s——t, Christopher. Life is way too hard. I might as well get out of here!"

Christopher drops Elliott of at home, and, as Elliott goes up the stairs, he gets a call from Rita. She has been a wonderful coach on a few occasions.

"Hey, Elliott, how are you?"

"Your timing is impeccable, Rita. I am about to off myself."

Rita starts laughing. "You are doing great. This is part of the awakening process."

"Seriously, this is part of the process?"

"Yes, Elliott, let go of everything. I have been in your shoes, and I also have been on the brink of suicide. But trust me, this is a necessary component. Everything is going perfect."

"Well, Rita, the process sucks. I am not liking it at all."

They talk for about thirty minutes, and it all makes sense eventually. Elliott is relieved that he was able to talk to Rita. Lesson learned. Every emotion is valid. Elliott has been taught to seek out joy and walk away from pain, misery, and agony. But they are both needed to enrich our lives. How can one appreciate the good if one has not experienced the bad? The trick is to experience it and embrace it as a wonderful experience by transcending the duality of our existence. Now that is easier said than done, but worth trying.

PALM SPRINGS MAGIC

HARMONIC UNIVERSE ONE. Twenty-First Century. Planet Earth.

Elliott is super-enthused when his good friend, Ken, swings by from Chicago for a whole week of vacation. The tension between him and his friends has been mounting over the few months, and many have left him as a consequence of him making no sense whatsoever. Ken has always listened carefully to what he has to say when they are talking over the phone, and their ten-year-old friendship is beaming as ever before. Ken is a yoga master and has been trying to awaken Elliott's spiritual life a few times in the past, but without much success. Unfortunately, that week it is rather chilly in San Diego, so they decide to go to Palm Springs to warm up. They find a quaint hotel, and soon they are lying by the pool, soaking up the bright yellow California sun.

"If you could set one intent for this week, what would it be?" asks Ken.

"I would love to experience unconditional love without having to be in Heaven. It is such a great feeling, and I want to feel it here when I am in a physical body."

"That is a great goal," says Ken. "I would settle for peace of mind."

At a certain point, Elliott feels the presence of an entity. He thinks it's Archangel Michael, but the energy is unlike what he has felt before, so he reaches out with his mind.

"*Who is here?*"

"*Elliott, it is me, Adrea.*"

"Adrea?" he gasps out loudly.

Adrea is Ken's wife who passed away from pancreatic cancer the year before. She and Elliott have been great friends for almost a decade.

Ken looks up quickly. "Did you say Adrea's name?"

"Adrea is here," Elliott says excitedly.

"She is? Really? Tell her I love her."

Adrea replies to Elliott, "*Tell Ken, I already know. Can you relay some other messages to Ken for me?*"

Elliott smiles in his mind. "*Yes, I can.*" And he turns to Ken first.

"Ken, you've got mail. Adrea wants you to give you a few messages. I will try and translate to the best I can."

"OK. I am all ears now," Ken says as he sits up from the pool chair.

Adrea continues, "*Tell him that I am glad that he donated all my clothes. But the green hat and the purple coat are still left, and I want him to give them away also.*"

"She wants you to also give away the green hat and the purple coat. Do not hold on to it."

"That is true, Elliott, yes. I was going to hold on to those. You could have never known that. My God, this is really happening."

Feeling confident, Elliott replies to Ken, "Yes, it is. Now that you confirmed that piece of information, I can trust the message a bit better. I only feel the presence. It could have been anyone. There are no identity cards on the other side, you know. At least not in a way that I can fully comprehend yet."

Adrea continues transferring messages through Elliott, and they are all confirmed by Ken. At a certain moment, Adrea says, "*Elliott, I can only see Ken and you as energy patterns, which is what you truly are. But I would love to see my husband one more time through human eyes and feel his skin on my skin. Would you mind if I use your body for a little while?*"

"*Oh, wow, Adrea, I've never done that. I need to check with Creator. Hold on.*"

Elliott links up with Creator, and he gets two thumbs up and a promise that He/She/It will oversee the process and make sure that all goes well.

"*All right, Adrea. I got the green light. So yes, I agree to you utilizing my body temporarily. But I have no clue as to how you are going to do that.*"

"*Just let me drive, Elliott. Close your eyes and enjoy the show.*"

Elliott feels a soft silken energy drape around and slowly entering him through the crown chakra. It feels almost like his body is being puffed up by a few inches, and he feels the energy slowly spiraling down like a cooling vapor. His consciousness expands beyond what he has ever experienced before, and he experiences multiple realities the same time, and he feels infinite unconditional love unfiltered. It was one of the best experiences he ever witnessed. Movies of river creeks, crystal clear water, being one with the water and the river bedrock, and the exquisite feeling of the water caressing the bedrock. Birds flying and feeling the air over their wings. Numerous colors swirling around in a misty substance, colors so bright and so opulent, they have not yet been discovered. He feels Adrea's consciousness and her love for him, and he feels a soothing smile that is fully appreciating at the same time. Adrea's consciousness gently takes over the control over his bodily functions. Elliott's eyes open, and Adrea sees Ken. A big smile appears on Elliott's face. From Elliott's perspective, it is like Adrea is at the steering wheel of a bus, and he is sitting behind her watching through the front windows, which are the boundaries of his eyes and consciousness.

Elliott femininely crosses his legs and puts his hand on Ken's knee. "*Ken, my husband, I love you so much. You have no idea. I came here to help you find peace. Because you still feel guilty about certain events that happened during our marriage. And I am here to tell you to let go of guilt. Because before we came here, before we reincarnate, we set up a plan with a whole bunch of loving Souls and the Creator of all love to experience what we want to experience. I wanted to learn forgiveness, because forgiveness cannot be experienced where I am right now. Everything here is in harmony. So I asked you beforehand if you loved me enough to betray me in our human lives and you agreed. You have betrayed me as many times as was needed for me to finally experience forgiveness fully. And I thank you for that. I finally experienced forgiveness, Ken. Thank you so much for all that you have done to me and for me. It is the most beautiful gift I could ever ask for. But now it is time to let go of your guilt. It does not serve you. It does not serve Griffin, our son. Be an example for him without being too overbearing. He is destined for great things. Tell him about our conversation.*"

"I will, Adrea. I will," replies Ken, and tears are streaming from his eyes.

And Adrea continues, "*Now, I want you to go to the hotel room and lie down in the bed. I will be there with you in a moment in spirit form, and I want you to open yourself to me so I can be fully with you. Do not worry about Elliott. We are interlinked, and he has agreed to stay here by the pool for as long as is needed. Do not worry about having to leave him behind. From now on, it is time for you. You have sacrificed so much of yourself, and you are still doing that. Teach Griffin to take care of himself by taking care of yourself first. You cannot be a light if you continue to give it away to others. Once your cup is running over, then you can start taking care of others. Elliott needs to learn that lesson too. It is like being in an airplane: put your oxygen mask on first and then serve the passengers next to you. I love you, Ken, unconditionally. I will always love you with all that I am.*"

Adrea leaves Elliott's body, and he is now fully aware of his surroundings. He looks at Ken, whose eyes are all puffy. Tears are running down his cheeks. "I guess I have to go to the room."

"Yes, you do, Ken. I will be waiting here," Elliott says patiently and knowingly.

Ninety minutes later, Ken returns to the pool with paper handkerchiefs in his hand. "Adrea told me to give these to you. She wants you to go to the hotel room and lie down. That was the most amazing experience I have ever had. I will tell you all about it later."

Elliott takes the handkerchiefs, walks to the room, and lies down in bed. Within a few minutes, Elliott feels Adrea draping herself around him, but not entering him completely.

"*Elliott, you are such an amazing person and a good friend to Ken. I have been asked to show you certain things, but are you ready to face yourself?*"

"*Yes, I am.*"

A wooden chest surrounded with chains appears in Elliott's mind. The chains are unfolding and being pulled away from the chest until it opens. The first figure he sees coming out of the chest is a double of himself but with thousands of nails and thorns driven through his skin from the inside out, and it is screaming in pain. Adrea speaks in his mind. "*This is your agony. Embrace it. Feel its pain and love it unconditionally. I will help you with that.*"

Elliott embraces the screaming twin and pulls him toward his chest. His body starts convulsing in the bed, and he screams out in pain. A soothing inflow of energy follows, and the pain subsides as Adrea soothingly whispers to him, "*You are going through an accelerated purification process. This will not be easy for you. Most people take lifetimes to do what you are trying to achieve in one lifetime. You have other selves that you are slowly becoming aware of. Your Soul is experiencing itself in many other facets in different time/space coordinates. One of which has hanged himself, and you linked up with that part of you a few days ago after Christopher made you doubt yourself at Moe's. Learn from it. Through your fast awakening you will experience discomfort. Please do not take your life in this human experience. We will be by your side all the way. The life-taking experience has already happened and will not nourish your Soul any further. You have so much to give and so much to teach. You came here to teach and to transform. Your heart has remained pure through all your ordeals, and your love for your Creator and your fellow men is enormous when measured on a human scale. Ask for help if things get too hard. You are never alone, but in the process of letting go, you may feel like you are alone. Many challenges lie ahead. Please know that you are always loved and guarded. Take good care of yourself. Be kind to yourself. Do not judge yourself, even when you think you are doing it wrong, because you are doing it right. That is the name of the game. That is what you will teach through example. To overcome adversity and still live in love for all that is, whether it is physically manifested or not. One last advice: learn discernment. Not all is what it seems like it is. You came here to experience betrayal, and it will be served to you in the most painful manner as you have requested. Do not judge the other or yourself if and when this happens. Forgive them because they do not know what they are doing, because they agreed to forget for your sake. This is all in service to one another. There is much love out there for you. Live, Elliott, live fully and without regrets, without shame, without doubt. Embrace it all and savor it. This is a gift, which will seem unbearable at times, but it is a gift that you set out for yourself. Love, Elliott, love unabashedly and teach the Sacred Law of One to all who are willing to listen. Because in the end, the only thing that is real is love. All else is an illusion. We are, you are, love and light. That is all we are. Good luck!"*

THE DOWNLOAD INTO THE ARTIFICIAL RECOVERY CYBORG

HARMONIC UNIVERSE FOUR. 3.8 Million AD. Planet Wakala.

Commander Jane Darkon is dressed in a white gown and is lying down on a white round table. Many of Dr. Brobol's assistants are running around, and a whole array of friends and family is watching from the second-level balcony as a support team for Jane's download into the artificial reality.

"So now that you understand that your reality is projected through the DNA and that your thoughts alter DNA, much like transcription factors in the molecular biology of the cell, we urge you to be careful what you think. Good thoughts equal statistically higher probabilities of good experiences and vice versa. You will remember this advice at certain points in your experience because we have hidden clues in your experience. For example, the flying horse Pegasus and the red dragon power animal will always be around you in energetic form. The Blue flame or the Blue Light will come up quite a few times, and the sky is blue as a very obvious, but to you in the artificial reality construct a not-so-obvious, reminder where you really came from. Once you start assembling what is going on, the artificial experience will be much easier for you. Any questions?"

"No, Dr. Brobol. I think we are good to go."

One of Dr. Brobol's assistants pushes a series of projected buttons on a light panel, and the entire round white table lights up. Jane is swiftly transported in a lucid dream state. In that state, her consciousness follows a bright white light and then encounters a yellow white light vehicle that looks like two counter-rotating pyramids with opposing tops and bottoms, a star tetrahedron or merkaba as some people call it. It feels like her consciousness is merging with the star tetrahedron but not entirely. She is aware that beings are working at her shoulder blade area, and it feels like weightless wings are being attached to the back.

"What is the status?" asks Dr. Brobol.

A young Vegan male, named Amadeus, answers. "Wave induced nodal grafts (WINGs) have been attached and are holding the original memory imprints for later recovery. Backing up from WINGs. Three. Two. One. Backup initiated."

"Great job, Amadeus!" says Dr. Brobol.

The star tetrahedron goes down and merges with the white light at table level. All goes white, then bright yellow-golden, and Jane sees the table she is lying on from above.

Amadeus continues, "Consciousness is uploaded into the streaming buffer. Adding therapy-specific energy patterns and adding the original consciousness energy patterns to the new ARC matrix."

"Prepare the ARC for download!" commands Dr. Brobol.

A three-dimensional movie is projected next to the circular table that Jane is lying on. The staff can see Elliott preparing for his meditation.

The table that Jane is lying on continues to light up. More and more blue-white light is streaming in from helical tubes attached to crystal generators. When all is stabilized, the entire table is transformed in a blue liquid light. From Jane's perspective, it appears that she is guiding many people through a portal to the other side; these represent the characters to her new movie. She is the last one to go through. She peeks in and sees a new world. The last memory that she holds becomes erased as she passes through. "I am coming back to be with my loved ones."

"Download completed, Dr. Brobol."

"Thank you, Amadeus."

Computer voice: "Warning! Matrix imbalance in the ARC. Warning!"

Dr. Brobol looks at the statistics, numbers, and graphs that are flashing on a multitude of projected screens. "It is a defunct algorithm that is being rejected in the core matrix. Jane's original memory patterns are taking over the original body design of the ARC."

Dr. Brobol shouts, "Bring up the four-dimensional control panel. We need to divert attention away from the pseudo-physical parameters to restore the ARC and successfully integrate Jane's consciousness. Computer, load negative feedback from ARC long-term memory into ARC awareness and start sequential temporary alignment for perception after core stability has been reached."

Computer voice: "Negative feedback from ARC long-term memory loaded. Temporal resolution in progress."

A few seconds later, the computer blurts: "Core matrix destabilizing in progress and accelerating."

Dr. Brobol fumes when he looks at the data. "The ARC is resisting. It is rejecting the new data. We need to go more drastic. I do not like doing this, but we have no choice."

And Dr. Brobol gives the command, "Computer, start environmental diversions programs 546 and 372. Start extreme pain program 67423. This should override the original consciousness and bring it down a notch. Then, bring the microphone online. And unmute the sound. I want to hear what the ARC is saying."

Computer voice: "Program 546 activated."

Water starts gushing out of the shower head in Elliott's bathroom.

Computer voice: "Program 372 activated."

In Elliott's reality, the toilet bowl suddenly starts having its own mind and decides to flush every two to five minutes. They can see Elliott running to the bathroom to fix the shower and the toilet bowl. And a few time intervals later, they notice Elliott running from the bathroom to the bedroom. He jumps on the bed and crawls in fetal position, crying.

Computer voice: "Virtual sound display activated."

And they hear the Elliott-ARC whispering, "This is not what I wanted. This is not what I wanted."

Computer voice: "Program 67423 activated."

"*Aaaaarrrrggghhhh!*" screams the Elliott-ARC. It feels like a laser beam is cutting open its left leg. "God, please make this stop. Please."

Dr. Brobol takes the microphone and speaks, "Elliott, we can help you with the pain. Do you want us to help you?"

"Yes, yes!" Elliott shouts painfully.

"Do you want to remember?" asks Dr. Brobol.

"No!" Elliott gasps. "Hold on! Wait a minute!"

Computer voice in the medical room: "Core matrix stabilized."

"I have changed my mind. I do not want to forget. Allow me to have these memories."

"Very well. And so it is," says Dr. Brobol and deactivates the microphone. "Computer, deactivate all ancillary programs prior to stabilization. Run a full-scale diagnostics."

"Programs deactivated." A few seconds pass. "All systems within parameters."

Dr. Brobol sighs, relieved. "That was a handful. Amadeus, can you recalibrate the ARC matrix?"

"Yes, Doctor. Recalibrating ARC matrix."

"Thank you, Amadeus. The ARC with Jane's consciousness will be in sleep mode on the other side to integrate and harmonize into her new surroundings. That gives us time for a break. Good work everyone!" Dr. Brobol leaves for the cafeteria.

THE WALK-IN EXPERIENCE

HARMONIC UNIVERSE ONE. Twenty-First Century. Planet Earth.

Elliott has been reading books after Archangel Michael's explanation of the ascension process. He is set on reaching fifth-dimensional consciousness so he can manipulate matter with the will of his mind.

He goes into meditation mode and proceeds to increase his vibration so he can experience something new. At least that is the intention that he sets.

Soon after, there is a lot of energy flowing in, and he sees white-and-yellow light and a merkaba-like structure. This process continues for quite a long time, and at a certain point he feels his body changing into a woman's body. This is not exactly what Elliott is looking for, and he starts panicking because of all these bodily changes. He tries to lie down and calm his mind, but the pain from his changing physiology and the confusion that goes along with it do not help with the calming of his mind.

Many images and impressions from his past are zooming in and out, and he is being faced with his worst fears, doubts, regrets, and mistakes in his life. They are all appearing right in front of him, and very clear in his mind. To face all your ugly sides in a few minutes and relive the awful feeling that comes with them is agonizingly painful. Meantime, he hears his shower starting to run, and soon after, his toilet bowl starts to flush repeatedly. He runs to the shower to stop the water, but he is unable to turn off the faucet. It just doesn't move. He can't fix the flushing toilet, and so he decides to turn off the main water valve. That does not stop the toilet from flushing or the water from running in the shower. Now he freaks out and runs to the bed. He's lying facedown, crying in his pillow.

"This is not what I wanted! This is not what I wanted!" he shouts.

A searing pain starts in his lower left leg. It feels like a laser is cutting in his bone and muscle for about eight inches in length and two inches in diameter. And it hurts. It hurts a lot, almost to the point of him passing out.

"*Aaaaarrrrggghhhh*!" he screams out, yelling in pain. He turns into the fetal position, crawled in like a ball. The pain doesn't stop but dulls after a few minutes. He pulls himself up by the bed board.

"God, please make this stop. Please."

He is now holding onto the bed board with two hands, and he is half standing up and half falling down while a voice out of nowhere states clearly, "We can help you with the pain. Do you want us to help you?"

"Yes, yes!"

"Do you want to remember?"

"No!" he gasps. "Hold on! Wait a minute."

Elliott's mind is thinking fast now. "*Do I really want to forget? And how much am I going to forget? Maybe better not to forget then*?"

He sighs out in a heavy voice, "I have changed my mind. I do not want to forget. Allow me to have these memories."

"Very well. And so it is."

A mantle of soothing energy envelops Elliott; the pain stops immediately, and he relaxes down into the bed. He feels a laser etching around his head and other body parts, and he falls into a deep sleep. A new consciousness enters his mind and takes over the body.

DR. BROBOL'S VILLA

HARMONIC UNIVERSE FOUR. 3.8 Million AD. Planet Wakala.

Dr. Brobol's light–sound vehicle is translucent in nature. His consciousness is linked to its vehicle through a neuro-adaptive interface, and he hovers safely above the crystal clear lake surrounded by lush green forests. When he lands the vehicle on the rooftop of his villa, it links with the photonic buffer unit, and when he steps out, he disengages the neural link and the light vehicle disappears into nothingness as it becomes absorbed by the photonic buffers.

He walks down the stairs to his office and finds an incoming secure message.

Dr. Brobol accepts the secure hyperspace channel, and a three-dimensional hologram appears in front of him. The caller identification indicates General H'Roc is online, and his yellow-green scales are displayed luminously in the three-dimensional hologram.

"Has Commander Jane Darkon been successfully transferred to the artificial reality?" General H'Roc barks ominously.

"Yes, she has," replies Dr. Brobol.

"Great job, Dr. Brobol. I am expecting the security codes, spatial time coordinates, grid coordinates, and frequency modulation ranges at my disposal shortly, correct?" says General H'Roc as his eyes glow yellower for an instant.

"Yes, I am sending them over, right now." And Dr. Brobol starts toggling fervently at the projected displays.

"We appreciate your cooperation, Doctor. We could not interfere in her recovery without your cooperation. But tell me. Why would you hand out this information so easily?"

"I have my reasons, General H'Roc. Suffice it to say that I am no longer willing to walk in the shadow of a woman who has forced me to give up a military career at the Intergalactic Federation. That's all you need to know."

"Revenge, Dr. Brobol, a beautiful, sweet, and noble emotion. You will enjoy watching the show. Rest assured, you will enjoy her scream at the top of her lungs. The Racoseta and the Geeray Rebellion are very grateful. You will be remembered as one of our heroes. Good-bye, Doctor."

SIGNS OR DECEPTIONS?

HARMONIC UNIVERSE ONE. Twenty-First Century. Planet Earth.

Elliott wakes up in a great mood. He notices there is something different, and it almost feels like there are two beings inside himself, the latter being extremely powerful and all-assuring. This great feeling continues the entire day, and he decides to test-drive his newfound confidence at a local dance club. There he meets Sheila, the ex-girlfriend of his friend Tony, and he tries to score with the nice-looking military nurse.

"Hey, Sheila, long time no hear. Where have you been?"

"Here and there, Elliott. Keeping busy. You know that you are a master, right?"

"A master? Then who are my subjects?" jokes Elliott evadingly.

"No, you're a spiritual teacher. You came here to teach and to transform."

"I have heard that before, yes. And how do you know that, Sheila? Have you been talking to Tony? He has been avoiding me, just so you know."

"Nope, I did not hear it from anyone, but I am like you, young one. I'm just further along the path. Tonight, I want you to bridge your heart chakra with your crown chakra, so your higher self can be anchored in your heart."

"I will take that advice to heart. Just to be sure you are not kidding. Am I living in *The Truman Show*? It really starts feeling like that in more than one way."

Sheila chuckles. "That is one way of looking at it. But you are right. Reality here is relative, and you are playing very well with the concepts. I am just here to bring a piece of advice. This is your first and last humanoid reincarnation, just so you know. After that you will want to explore life as a tree and as a dolphin, even though both of them are happening simultaneously. Time does not exist the way most people here believe it does. You remember that, right?"

"Yes, I do, Sheila, and I have seen how relative time can be here and there."

"Correct, because the time relationship or relativity depends on the difference between the particle pulsation speed and the rotational angle of the particles that your consciousness is moving through."

"How did you become so smart so suddenly, Sheila? You did not talk about this when you were with Tony."

"Because you were not ready then. I see now that you are eager to learn more. Next up for you is to learn to connect with all that is around you at all times. There are twenty-two people on this patio, not including us, and I know that without having to count. I just know, because I am them and they are me, just like you are me and I am you. Once you master this skill, you are well on your way to the so-called ascension. Then you can start teaching what you have experienced. Until then, work on yourself and try to keep a low profile. I will tell you one more secret: the key is water," Sheila says while nodding and smiling.

Elliott scratches his head. "OK, I will try and remember all that. That is a handful. You want to grab a drink?"

"No, Elliott, your buddy Beckster wants to talk to you."

Elliott looks around the patio. "I have not seen Beckster yet. Have you?"

"He is waiting in line to get in. That is one of the perks of being dialed-in. You just know who is where and why. Enjoy your evening." And Sheila turns around and leaves the premises.

Ten minutes later, Elliott runs into Beckster. "Hey, Beckster, good to see you."

"Hey, Elliott, look what I got. Two cosmos and four shots of tequila. Want to share these with me?"

"I am not so sure, Beckster. Do you think that is really a good idea?"

"Look, Elliott, for so many months you have been very sober, and I did not complain, but now I want you to have some fun with me. Share the experience with me. Please?"

"All right, fine. Let's go to the patio."

Elliott walks to the patio and finds a place to sit down while Beckster is held up by one of his friends. Suddenly he sees the Virgin Mary right in front of him.

"*Elliott, what are you doing?*"

Elliott rolls his eyes and replies rashly, "*Well, apparently I'm not drinking these shots and cosmos anymore, since you are asking.*"

Calmly and lovingly the Virgin Mary replies, "*No, you either take it or you don't. It doesn't really matter, because matter doesn't really exist. Unless you make it matter. And your energy is making it matter in split ways. There is one part of you that would love to enjoy a great night dancing with Beckster and another part is feeling guilty over ingesting this substance. From our side, this is all good. Remember, unconditional love. We want you to enjoy your life fully. So if you are going to take the drinks with the underlying intention of fear or guilt or shame, please do not take them. If your intention is to enjoy and loosen up a little, please go ahead and enjoy. Let go of the guilt. I have blessed the drinks to transmute some of its frequencies. Transmutation is a skill we will teach you as you grow. Go ahead, take the blessed drinks and have fun. We are all rooting for you.*"

"*If you say so.*" And he swallows down the shots of tequila.

Beckster is standing by him in the meantime. "Are you having those talks in your head again? Really? Here?"

"I had a run in with the Virgin Mary. All good now. Let's dance!"

Beckster rolls his eyes. "Your stories, Elliott. Sometimes too much to handle." He grabs Elliott by the shoulder and off they go. Tiesto's "Blessed" is blasting through the speakers, but neither Elliott nor Beckster notice the fine detail in synchronous music selection.

I get a little stressed out,
Every now and then,
But problems come,
And problems go,
When I'm around him,
Blessed in the morning,
Blessed in the evening,
And again, I realize he reason why I sing,

Blessed, blessed, blessed, blessed, blessed,
Blessed, blesses, blessed, blessed, blessed . . .

While the song is playing, Elliott acknowledges the presence of Archangel Michael, who continues to teach by whispering in his mind.

"*The only thing that needs to happen is to educate the population on the mechanics of energy and the illusory perception of reality. You may want to consider that your reality is artificial from the perspective of other beings. There are Souls who came into this artificial reality for many different reasons, and one has recently been downloaded in your perceptual human body construct.*"

Elliott gasps. "*Is that what happened to me? Is that why I feel a secondary presence in my being?*"

And the archangel replies, "*Yes and no. There is a lot more going on at many levels, and you will live it out as part of a galactic movie. For now, let's just say that you have agreed to be in service to the healing of a wonderful being. It is all part of a plan that many call ascension. Many Souls are aware of the importance of this event, and some decide to shed their bodies through orchestration of accidents or mass exits like catastrophes, because they think they can evolve faster when out of the body. This is described in some of your text books as revelation. I have hinted this to you many months ago at the dance floor.*"

"*No way!*" Elliott utters, surprised. "*The ascension is really happening?*"

"*It has started millions of years ago, and for the next five to ten years you will see the culmination of it. Your three-dimensional reality is currently the best reality TV in the entire cosmos. Many species are watching to see what happens to humanity, and there are a few who do not wish your evolution into divinity.*"

"*Who are the species that do not wish this evolution?*"

"*There are more than a few. But you will meet these so-called bad ones more acutely in a manner that you would not expect. I invite you to prepare accordingly and start assembling your higher DNA strands so that you are less vulnerable to subliminal manipulation and flat out behavioral regulation.*"

"*Fair enough,*" thinks Elliott, and then wonders. "*How do I build my DNA?*"

"*That is something that will come to you in a vision. I have told you much that you need to integrate, or not if you do not wish to do so. Until the next time. Much love to you, Elliott.*" And Archangel Michael disappears.

FATE OR CREATING DESTINY?

HARMONIC UNIVERSE ONE. Twenty-First Century. Planet Earth.

In the middle of the night, Elliott is awakened by Creator: "*Elliott, do you want to learn more?*"

"*Yes, please. Can you teach me whether our fate is set or whether we create our own destiny?*"

"*That is a great question, and the answer is both. Try to see life as a coloring book. The images have already been printed, and it is up to you to fill in the colors. This means that certain things are supposed to happen in your life, and others are optional per your choice. Free will, or better, how you react to a given circumstance is up to you. You see, life is like a CD-ROM of an entire video game. All your possible moves are already known beforehand. In the game you can decide to cross the narrow bridge or the broad bridge. You can decide to fight your foes, be defeated by your foes by not fighting, or avoid the confrontation. Sometimes you are forced in confrontation due to circumstances, and sometimes you are not. This is all decided before you come to live here on this planet, between you and Me and a whole array of support that will come with you or stay behind the scenes. It is also meant as a test to see if you fully understand during your life experience that we are all One. If you act like the other is unlike yourself and you do things to that being that you would not possibly do to yourself, then you get to play the role of the one being suppressed the next time you decide to play in the game. It is all fair. There are beings who still do not believe this reality, but they are painstakingly mistaken to think that this is not true, and they are, in fact, through their thoughts and actions, punishing themselves, which they see as others. Now there are those who come in with some advantages in the game such as yourself. You have a larger array of DNA strands than the average person, with the burden of responsibility to assemble these fully as you go on with your life. It is a give-and-take. Your presence allows me to send ultrahigh frequencies through your ethereal body and for you to transmit it in your relative reality. You could say that you are a beacon of light. There are many beings such as yourself, and it is up to you to decide whether you want to help these others or not. As you are writing this down, your words, My words, are helping them grow into the embodiment that they were meant to be.*

"To understand the reality of fate versus destiny, I also ask you to consider that they are always two opposing forces needed. Much like a brake and an accelerator in a car. For instance, heat and cold are two opposing forces. Love and fear is another example. The opposite of balance is deviation. The opposite of fate is creating destiny. All these forces are intricately linked to one another to create harmony at any given moment in time. It is impossible to go wrong, because it has already been calculated beforehand.

"Another thing I want you to consider is that this Universe is fractal in nature. I will explain the Tree of Life and the Tree of Knowledge and how they are interlinked and contribute to the fractal Universe at a different time. Just know that this Universe is fractal in nature, so if you want to know what is going on in the galaxy, just take a look at your planet. Yes, there is a galactic war going on, and you are at the center of the movement. Remember that unconditional love is the unifier. It is the starting key from the first movement, which I will explain in more detail. In your experience, love has a certain frequency pattern and fear has another frequency pattern. However, they are only *frequencies perceived to be pleasant or unpleasant depending on how you were designed or trained to think, or both. Some of these fear frequencies I have built in. For example, I programmed toxic leaves or fruits with a bad taste so that you would not eat them. But taste is only a perceptual realization of a frequency. The frequency of fear of an electron for another electron is much higher than it is for you, because an electron is so much smaller than you are. Fear is the perception of repelling forces because two probability functions come together, and when they are annihilating in nature, they collapse each other fully or partially. When two probability functions come together, and they are additive, they amplify each other fully or partially. Fear is diminishing or annihilating in nature. Love is additive.*

"Now let's go back to creating matter. Take a bunch of magnetic balls. You got them? OK, the ground rule is that all forces and matter are created from the center, and we strive for equality and balance as much as possible. Also, the closer they stay together, the stronger they are. That is another guideline. The exception is the first movement, which we have covered in detail elsewhere. To create the third magnetic ball, imagine the two magnetic balls separating and a third one growing in size to the same size as the other balls. The third ball will move upward or downward so that a triangle is formed, an equilateral triangle. The fourth ball starts forming in the middle of the triangle, and when it is grown to the same size as the others, it forms a tetrahedron. This is the strongest platonic three-dimensional shape known to man. Diamonds have a tetrahedron shape and are merely carbon atoms bonded together. Pencils are merely carbon atoms too, but the three-dimensional bonds have not formed. So the two-dimensional layers slide over one another, and you can draw with this so-called graphite on paper as it leaves the layers behind. Under the pressure of the Earth's crust and with heat, the diamond is formed. Similarly, much strength and sacrifice was needed to create the first tetrahedron. The fifth ball emerges in the center of the tetrahedron and will move into a position to create a hexagon. The sixth sphere will start forming in the middle of the triangle. The sixth ball will keep forming, eventually pushing up balls four and five, but statistically it is more probable that ball five is pushed away and then it rotates. There is a temporary separation of ball five from the group of balls before the ninety-degree angular rotation between all spheres, not only spheres four and five, although spheres four and five experience the most rotational and vibrational effects, which are felt in sphere one through three and cushioned downwards. Imagine a pudding or gelatin settling after you poked it. Once you have the sixth sphere in place, you can have rotation around the axis between spheres three and four. Depending on when the next sphere forms, two possible configurations are possible: two opposing tetrahedrons held together by one connecting sphere or a five-star shape with two outwardly pushed spheres in the middle. This in your language can be seen as the point where fate versus destiny is decided, because it leads to two very different structures on an energetic level and, as such, on a physical level. It is like choosing between fear and love. So the choice is up to you. Do you wish to experience fear? Then think fear, and it will predominantly manifest from your energetic output in your physical manifest reality. Or, if you chose love, you will manifest different reality structures that are more

aligned with love. There is the choice for you. Creating your destiny versus relying on fate. At the same time, also be aware of the fractal nature of the Universe. You may have control over a few wheels in let's say a Swiss watch, but you do not have control over all the wheels. And with that, we end up to the beginning of the answer to your question. There is both fate and creating destiny."

THE ANCIENTS RETURN

HARMONIC UNIVERSE TWO. 75,000 BC. Lemuria. Planet Earth.

After the connection with the Ancients was so suddenly interrupted, Kurt has been concerned about current and future events. He remembers fully well a piece of information that was not shared with the council members, but he just can't put his mind to it. Most likely the Ancients have withdrawn that missing piece from his memory, yet he remembers very well the feelings he experienced right before the transmission was interrupted: deep betrayal, pain, fear, and confusion.

As a result of these lingering feelings and to find peace within, he travels to the Black Table Mountain, a mountain range outside of the city. When he arrives at the Sacred Ground, he prepares for an audience with the Ancients by placing onyx, quartz, hematite, citrine, and amethyst crystals in a pentagram coordination along the edges of a circle drawn with his staff, which carries a blue sapphire in the middle along with other precious and semiprecious stones. Many old runes and symbols are edged into the gold-silver plating of the crystalline staff. He walks around the circle and taps each crystal with the top of the staff, and the crystals activate. A luminous hue surrounds them, and an audible zooming hum can be heard from the activated crystals. Kurt steps into the circle and starts the incantation part of the ceremony while holding the tip of the staff in the northern direction.

"I call upon the Guardian of the Northern Tower." A pillar of a cyclonic air column appears out of nowhere. Winds gust at the Sacred Grounds, and the Golden Ephesian Bow hovers in the middle of the air column, shining bright white-and-golden light. And Kurt continues, now facing the south.

"I call upon the Guardian of the Southern Tower." A stone column erects itself from the ground up; the earth around is shaking tremors, and a rumbling sound surrounds the Sacred Grounds. A rune engraved metal-like hammer hovers above the column, and lightning flashes from the hammer and around the column. Kurt seems unfazed and turns his gaze to the west.

"I call upon the Guardian of the Western Tower." Water starts spouting from the ground, raindrops fall down in the middle of gusting winds, and there are flashes of lightning and rumblings of thunder. A pillar of water appears, and in the middle a silver-palladium spear appears. And at the tip of the spear a red sphere lights up and activates the symbols that are engraved in the metal crystalline tip; they light up as if a silver fire is turning them on one by one. Kurt turns to the east side and shouts over the tempest.

"I call upon the Guardian of the Eastern Tower." Lightning strikes at the east side, and a pillar of fire and molten lava bubbles up from the floor, and in the middle, a crystalline sword with four wings of fire rotating around its vertical axis lights up in a blue haze, and many symbols light up on the sword in yellow-and-red fire patterns. At the Sacred Grounds the air feels hot and cold, humid and dry, and the ravaging forces of nature pound the grounds at full force.

Remarkably, in the Sacred Circle, Kurt is unaware or untouched by this show of magnificence that no one would be able to survive. Kurt pulls his staff in two and points one to the ground and one to the sky while exclaiming loudly and determinedly, "With the power of the Guardians combined, I call upon the alpha and the omega, the above and the below, the Creator and the un-Creator, the created and the uncreated, the yes and the no, the unifier and the divider. I ask for an audience with the Ancients for the benefit of all kind existing, existed, and to be."

The effect of these words is astounding: winds gusting, lightning striking, thunder rolling, and water and fire pellets gushing around in a crescendo as a yellow phoenix from above and a red phoenix from below combine in the Sacred Circle, creating a denser and denser golden fire around Kurt, and once these firebirds combine, the forces of nature subside immediately as if it never happened. From the outside, there seems to be a blazing fire where the Sacred Circle used to be. The fire flickers a few times and then disappears. The scenery is as beautiful and picturesque as before, and Kurt is nowhere to be found. It is eerily silent.

From Kurt's perspective, the fire surrounding him slowly fades away, and he finds himself looking at a completely different night sky firmament; he feels he is at the edge of the galaxy. The ground he stands on feels different, gravity feels different, and there seems to be no atmosphere; yet he is able to breathe. Graciously, two creatures—Ancients—float toward him, and he feels loved and cared for beyond anything he has ever experienced before. They look tall with eyes that look like the night sky and with wide white robes with gold and silver symbols embroidered in blue-banded sleeves.

The Ancients speak in unison. "Good day to you, our dearest beloved."

"Good day to you, Ancient Ones," says Kurt and he bows, upon which the Ancients bow to him.

The Ancients continue, "You have come far, and we are eager to meet you, Holy One."

"Holy One?" Kurt replies, surprised.

"Yes, Holy One," say the Ancients. "Allow us to continue. The sum of the whole is less than The One, until the whole is united. Why do you think that is? So we all strive to the common goal eventually, as we learn the Divine Truth. We all play a role. Nothing is trivial or happens by accident. Your role is to bring peace across many dimensions and in the physical expression of 'it'. It is written that He/She/It will walk over mountains. As the wind blows over Him, the Egg is crushed and the Seed of Life is spoiled many times over at the feet of those the He loves. And when He can bear no longer, He reaches for The Other Star. Many will name IT wrongly because That Star is more than what-can-be conceived. His love for Her, Her love for Him, love so deep, so pure, pleasure edges pain and begs many times, many pleas from father to daughter, like egg white to the egg yolk begging to serve as the ingredients for a Divine Meal, not knowing as ingredients, that the meal was planned before the chicken hatched The Egg for Her. Remember these words. They are important for You and many others."

Kurt is baffled. "I came here to inquire about what transpired before your transmission was interrupted."

And the Ancients respond, "That was not an accident. We were forced to disconnect because we ourselves experienced a transmission that was beyond ourselves. This transmission originated from deep within you and allowed us to experience existence beyond the cyclic nature of this Universe and as such beyond our immortality, which created fear and confusion on our behalf and a level of insight into the beginning and ending of this Universe, which cannot be told until that time is due. Deep betrayal hides within truth and lies, and you will bring this message to so-called humanity and beyond when the time is ripe."

"When will that be? How will I know what to say?" asks Kurt.

"The exact timing cannot be determined. We can only tell you that after a specific date, numerically coded as 12-12-12, no one except The One can predict what will happen across the entire galaxy. Through the breaking of the cycles, the fate and destiny of this Universe will change completely. We cannot see beyond that date, and many events surrounding these time and space coordinates are unclear. You will experience betrayal, pain, and suffering beyond what can be sustained because of what others imagine what carries you forward. This is not an easy path, Holy One, and it is what it will be and what yet is to be according to the Law of the Most High. Only You will know as you remember what you forgot, and we will forget for Our Sake. Remember to remind us, Holy One."

"Is there anything that I can do to prepare?" asks Kurt.

"The events we speak of will happen in one of your other lives in what many see as an ungodly way of living. You can prepare by making sure that you are surrounded by your closest friends, allies and enemies so to speak. The One that is to be needs to be protected until the day of remembrance for our sake. A happy human descendant will bring an end to the enslavement of many, and the message that can be carried through lineage should not be revealed to anyone but the Self by the Self."

"In that case, I could prepare by connecting with my future self that happens to be The One?" utters Kurt.

Patiently, the Ancients reply, "Yes and no. It will be helpful to a certain extent, but beyond the end of cycles, there is nothing we can accurately determine, and we can only assume that it will be the same for you. What we can tell you is that your plane of existence has a

Creator, and that Creator has a Creator and so on. Our Creator is not the same as your Creator. But beyond the cascades of Creators, there is the Unknown Creator sometimes referred to as Prime Creator or The One or All-That-Is. Much speculation surrounds the Unknown Creator, The One that created and uncreated all that is. The One that started and ended all that is, who always starts and always ends and never started and never ended. Who or what is beyond comprehension. To the best of our abilities, we surmise that the breaking of the cycles will occur by direct intervention through Prime Creator and/or a vessel thereof. You eventually will become or not that vessel through sacrifice of one of our known most highs."

Baffled, Kurt asks, "Me? A vessel for Prime Creator? Is that even possible?"

"While in the relative not all is possible and yet it may be so, from our relative absolute perspective all is possible in the absolute, per our projections from a previously infinite yet limited perspective. You will know as you go along your journey, and we will follow You on that path. Good-bye, Holy One." And the Ancients bow to Kurt, and the whole scenery disappears. The unknown night sky turns into a blue sky, and Kurt is back at the Sacred Circle, with many more questions than answers.

THE SEPARATION

HARMONIC UNIVERSE ONE. Twenty-First Century. Planet Earth.

After meeting another so-called master at the dance club, Elliott decides to take that advice to heart and sets his intention to bridge his crown and heart chakra during the meditation. When he lies down and closes his eyes, he can feel that other presence within him that seems to calm and comfort him. That other presence feels female in nature and imbues a level of confidence that he has not experienced before. During the meditation though, that consciousness seems to draw him further from his body, and he experiences a light show like never seen before. Suddenly he becomes aware of another body—a female body.

Meantime in Dr. Brobol's facility, many of his staff are on high alert.

"Prepare for upload of Commander Jane Darkon. Her body is out of bio-stasis and ready to accept her consciousness," shouts Dr. Brobol.

"Dr. Brobol, the ARC is in meditative trance state. Its body is unable to move. We are isolating and uploading the recovered consciousness of Commander Jane Darkon. It will take a while to sort that out."

"Very well, continue. Keep me posted," he replies to Amadeus, one of his technicians.

Computer voice: "Upload and isolation in progress 60 percent complete."

In Elliott's meditation, he feels a pull upward, and he becomes aware of a large room with many beings around him, and he hears, "Upload and isolation in progress, 60 percent complete" from a computerized voice.

Amadeus notices that something is wrong.

"Dr. Brobol, many parasitic algorithms are being uploaded with Jane Darkon's consciousness. They are not part of who she is. What do you recommend?"

Dr. Brobol looks at a whole string of data and graphs that are projected in front of him; he thinks for a few seconds to diagnose the cause and replies.

"A portion of the ARC is being uploaded as well. We cannot allow this to happen. It would disable the ARC and tamper with Jane's normal functioning. Map the parasitic algorithms to the original design of the ARC, extract them, and reroute them to the ARC. Execute program 6759 in addition to the reroute. That should help."

"Yes, Dr. Brobol. Uhm, that program is heavily encrypted, and I don't know what it will do. Are you sure you want me to use that?" says Albert.

"Yes, I have written that program specifically for this purpose. You will see. I wrote it myself and triple-checked it."

"OK."

Computer voice: "Program 6759 activated. Reroute initiated."

In Elliott's meditation, he feels like he is partially inside a different body, and suddenly he is pulled out and he feels being stripped away from the comforting consciousness that was within and around him. He feels her becoming aware of her surroundings, and like a Siamese twin being separated from his other half, slowly that connection is being severed. And he feels like two heads are separated from one another at the crown, like when two bodies are on two tables, and one table is rotated away. He wants to hold on and live in the comfort of togetherness, but he cannot stop the course of action. He faintly recognizes the other body waking up and remembering a life in an unknown galaxy, which is not his life, and then he becomes aware of his own body lying in bed in meditation. The feeling of abandonment is overwhelming, and he cries out in painful solitude. He is alone in bed and cries himself to sleep.

Meantime, four million years in the future, Commander Jane Darkon is awake and greeted by her family and friends, which she slowly recognizes as her consciousness becomes more and more fully aware of what transpired. "Oh my God, I'm back. That was rather short."

"Yes," replies Dr. Brobol. "Most of your traumas were healed during the ARC's dream state. You are lucky. That and there was an urgent need to pull you out. You were in danger."

"In danger?" questions Jane.

"Yes, we will put you in a memory retrieval unit now so you become reacquainted with all that you are and some of the things that you have voluntarily agreed to forget on behalf of many. You are a hero, Jane," says Dr. Brobol.

"What happens to the ARC? It felt like a real human being with hopes and dreams and desires. I remember that."

"The ARC is merely an artificial construct. From our perspective I would not call it alive."

"I'm not sure I agree with that, Dr. Brobol. I felt its pain and desolation when we separated. These artificial beings as you call them, they have thoughts and feelings too, just like we do."

"Let's have this discussion when you are in full remembrance of who you are. Albert, can you escort Commander Darkon to the memory retrieval unit? I will finish the report. And please do a full calibration on the ARC afterwards."

Albert responds excitedly, "Yes, Dr. Brobol."

A SINISTER PLAN

HARMONIC UNIVERSE THREE. 3.8 Million AD. Earth Solar System.

The *Ragnar* is a starship belonging to the Geeray. It is a Class V warship and houses the most innovative technological designs, and as such, it could be considered their flagship. At the bridge of the *Ragnar* starship, General H'Roc is informing his team of officers about his strategy.

"Gentlemen, we have been given the access and encryption codes to an artificial reality in which commander Jane Darkon's consciousness has been downloaded for the purpose of recovery from post-traumatic stress disorder. Needless to say, this is an ideal opportunity to get access to classified information about the Intergalactic Federation and its allies. And as a bonus, we get to play God with Commander Darkon and make sure that her trauma levels will be increased rather than reduced. From what I hear, she is coupled to an Artificial Recovery Cyborg (ARC) named Elliott Himmerept in that artificial reality, which is helping with her recovery. Our engineers have created a similar artificial reality to the one that the ARC is living in now. We will disconnect the ARC from its original operating system and upload it in our artificial reality, during which time the ARC and, as a consequence, Commander Jane Darkon will be completely under our control. During that time, we will have to work diligently to localize the access and encryption protocols. Through decrypting specific Keylontian codes, we can find out how to best target the Intergalactic Federation and their fleet starships. In order for the upload to succeed, we have to get as close as possible to Planet Wakala, which is why the *Ragnar* has been sent, because we have the most advanced cloaking device to make ourselves undetectable when in orbit around the planet. Once in orbit, we can establish a secure link with the artificial reality through the access codes, locate the ARC, and upload the ARC when it is in sleep mode. Any questions?"

Lieutenant Gord answers worriedly, "That is quite an undertaking. I'm sure we will remain cloaked during our journey through Intergalactic Federation space. Once we have uploaded the ARC, I am guessing they will notice that the ARC is missing. They will be able to trace our presence or trajectory by following our hyperspace signal. Are we ready for their response?"

General H'Roc scoffs at him. "By the time they notice that the ARC with Jane Darkon is missing, we will be far away from Federation space and surrounded by our fleet as well as our other allies, the Racoseta. We will be safe there, and we will have a strategic advantage. On our voyage back, the Federation will focus on the *Ragnar* for the purpose of retrieving Commander Darkon, while we will transmit ways to destroy their fleet ships to our collaborators before they have time to think or act. The Federation ships in pursuit of the Ragnar and off-world Federation planets will be targeted in coordinated attacks by our armadas. They will not even know what hit them and how we could destroy them so easily. Victory is ours!"

And the officers shout aloud, "Hail to the Queen! Hail Rak'El."

General H'Roc continues, "Very well then. Set a course for planet Wakala and remain cloaked for the entire duration of the journey. Let me know when we have arrived. I will be in my cabin. Adjourned."

THE EMISSARY IN ACTION

HARMONIC UNIVERSE ONE. Twenty-First Century. Planet Earth.

After the painful separation, Elliott decides to visit Europe with his partner Josie, just to keep his mind on the reality that he lives in. They have wanted to see the Netherlands, France, and Spain for quite a long time. In fact, traveling is one of their favorite hobbies. The night before their early morning departure to Schiphol, they are both packing their bags, when suddenly Elliott senses the presence of Archangel Michael, and while listening with his mind, he hears, "*Elliott, please go to the Silver Rail tonight. Your assistance is requested.*"

Elliott responds, "*Dude, we are getting ready to travel to Europe. Going to a bar is not in our plans tonight. Are you sure you need me there?*"

"*Yes, please.*"

"*OK, what do you want me to do there?*"

"*You will meet the right people when it is time, and you will know what to say.*"

"*Oh, come one, I do not like it when you are acting all mysterious. But OK, I will go there tonight when I finish packing my bags. Just so you know, I have to get up at six tomorrow morning. Perhaps I will meet you at the Silver Rail tonight?*"

"*Yes, you will, dear Elliott,*" replies Archangel Michael and disappears from the scene.

Later that night, at around 10:00 pm, Elliott arrives at the Silver Rail, and he walks in while reaching out to the other side.

"*Hey, Michael, are you here?*"

And he hears in his mind, "*Yes, I am.*"

"So what do you want me to do here?"

"Relax, Elliott, enjoy the journey. It is not all about the end result, because if that is your main expectation, then you will be unhappy many times more while on your way to the end result."

Elliott walks to the bar and orders a beer for him and Josie. Once he has been served, Josie takes him to the patio, which is packed with people. And that on a Monday night. To his right side stands a lady with her back to him, and he just feels the energy within him surging and he knows exactly what is going on. He taps her on the shoulder and introduces himself.

"Hi, my name is Elliott."

And she replies in a friendly manner, "Hi, I'm Jessica."

"This may sound strange to you, Jessica, but I have a message for you."

"You do?"

"Yes, I do. You have a most precious gift. You have the ability to see and diagnose disease without the use of x-rays or other radiological equipment. It is something that scares you because you do not understand it yet, and you are just discovering this part of yourself. But do not be afraid of it. Nurture it and embrace it. You can do many good things with this gift, you see?"

"Oh my God. How do you know that? Yes, it is true. I see these things in people, and I am actually studying to become a radiologist. I'm in the navy now. Yes, you are right. It scares me because I know what is going to show up on the screen before the patient is even in front of the machine. I'm just afraid of being labeled crazy. I thought I was going crazy, or maybe I had a brain tumor or so."

"Jessica, you are not going crazy, and you do not have a brain tumor either. This is really happening. My gift is to be a messenger and an equalizer, and I have been where you are now. Believe that what I say is true. There are many gifted people on this planet, and we came here in service to the others. Continue your education as a radiologist. It will help you better diagnose what is going on with your patients."

"I do. I do believe you. I just needed someone to tell me that. Thank you so much, Elliott!"

Meantime, Josie is watching the scene, and she leans into Elliott's ear.

"Another miracle?"

"Yes, another one."

And she replies, "When will these guys from the other side start paying you for taking up your time? I do exist too, remember? Don't get me wrong. I think it is great that you are able to help people. It's fascinating to watch. But you and I have a life too, and I wish that could be honored a little bit more. That is all."

"Don't worry, Josie. I'm not going to abandon our life here. That said, I do enjoy delivering these messages. In the beginning, I did not trust this gift, but now I just let it come and voila, instant miracle."

A VISIT TO ELLIOTT'S GRANDMOTHER

HARMONIC UNIVERSE ONE. Twenty-First Century. Planet Earth.

When in Europe, Elliott and Josie set out to visit his grandmother who lives in a hospice a few miles away from his parents' home. His grandmother, Maria, lost her husband a few years ago to Alzheimer's, and she needs a bit more medical care because of a cerebral stroke a few years ago, which paralyzed portions of her right side, including her arm.

When with his grandma, Elliott excitedly tells about his life in California and a few of the wonderful stories that he experienced in his awakening. His grandma listens carefully to every word he says, even though she is a bit hard of hearing. After about fifteen minutes, Elliott senses the presence of a spirit, and when he focuses his conscious mind for a bit, he hears, "*Elliott, it is me, your grandfather.*"

"*You are? Can you tell me about my youth and our visits?*" Elliott replies with his mind. He does that to verify whether the information he is receiving is correct and not some other spirit who just wants to play a bit. His grandfather starts telling him about his youth years in a very specific manner, and pretty soon, Elliott trusts that the information that is coming through is truly from his grandfather. And his grandfather continues, "*Put your hands on Grandma's shoulders, so I can be with her. You know you are a transmitter and while you are reconnected to the other side, she is still rather disconnected, but through you, I can be with her for a while.*"

"OK, Grandpa. I have to explain this to Grandma first."

And Elliott gently smiles to his grandmother while he interrupts Josie talking about their visit to Amsterdam.

"Grandma, your husband is here. And he would like to be with you more closely. Remember the stories I just told you about being a channel and a messenger? He asked me to put my hands on your shoulders so he could be with you. Are you OK with that?"

"Really? My dear husband is here? Oh, how I would love to be with him. Can you really do that?" asks grandma.

"Yes, I can," replies Elliott, and he gets up and walks behind her.

"Grandma, close your eyes and just relax. This will be a wonderful experience." And Elliott places his hands on her shoulders. Within seconds, he feels a gentle but vast stream of energy coming from above his head and moving within and around his arms, and the flow of energy envelops his grandmother. A huge smile appears on her face, eyes still closed, and her face changes into a face of joy and happiness. A few utterances of ohs and ahs escape her lips, and she is in bliss. A few tears roll down her cheek, but they are tears from happiness. The wonderful experience lasts more than a few minutes, and while this is happening, Elliott hears his grandfather talk.

"*Tell her to start writing again. It will bring her pleasure in her life here. Tell her to write about her experience as a way to help children. I will help her write. Please ask the attending nurse for a pen, and I will write for her.*"

Soon after, the energy flow fades away, and both Elliott and his grandma open their eyes. The first words that come out of Grandma's mouth are "That . . . was . . . the . . . most beautiful . . . experience . . . I have ever had. How did you that?"

"I just know, Grandma. I can't explain it. I do have a message from Grandpa, though. He wants you to write your life experience, which will help a lot of children."

"Oh, Elliott, I am too old for that, and I can't use my right hand anymore. That and I would not be able to read what I write. I can only read big letters, you know. I don't have my reading glasses anymore."

"Hold on," says Elliott as he runs out into the hall to the nurses' station. He grabs a pen at the desks and hurries back to the room where Josie and Grandma are waiting to see what comes next. When he gets back to the room, he wheels his grandma to the table and quickly grabs one of the newspapers, which are stacked in a pile by the wardrobe closet. As he is holding the pen in front of grandma, he exclaims joyfully.

"Try and write something. Anything. It doesn't matter what. Grandpa said he would help you."

And the eighty-four–year-old woman puts the pen in her left hand and bends over so she can write on the paper. She looks for a bit of open space in between the paragraphs, and miraculously she is writing, albeit very slowly. When she is done, Elliott tries to determine whether she actually wrote a legible sentence or plain old gibberish. And while he reads, his eyes grow wide open.

"I am good here with Grandma" is what she wrote. He decides not to tell her what he just read, but he takes a picture anyway.

After the visit, Josie and Elliott return to his parents' home for dinner. As soon as they get in, he tells his father what happened with Grandma, and he shows him the picture. His dad has been a staunch unbeliever and relies on logic mainly. When his father reads the sentence "I'm good here with Grandma," he does question why Grandma would be writing that sentence, and he wanders to his office. Soon after, he comes back with a whole binder of letters and documents.

"These are letters and affidavits from the finances that I used to run for your grandparents. And I know that what she wrote is not her handwriting," says Elliott's dad.

He pulls out a sheet and starts comparing the handwritings. Very quickly the truth is revealed, and the unbelieving father admittedly utters, "This can't be! It is your grandfather's handwriting."

Meantime, Elliott's mother has entered the living room to see what all the excitement is about. She is quickly informed about the happenings with Grandma and the newfound evidence that what Grandma wrote is Grandfather's handwriting.

"Well, that is a coincidence," says Elliott's mom, and continues, "You know what today is, right?"

"No, not really."

"Today is the anniversary of the day your grandfather died. And look, you see where Grandma wrote in between the paragraphs for the newspaper. Look at the printed name of the author, right below Grandma's writing. It reads 'Franciscus.' That is your grandfather's name."

Josie blurts out, "No way. Wow! Maybe it was really Grandpa in the room."

Needless to say that Elliott's parents were taking his newfound experiences a bit more seriously. They used to brush them aside as rubbish, and quite honestly, they have urged him to go see a psychiatrist more than once. Now they are reconsidering that something else might be going on. Elliott is happy when he leaves his parents' home with this insight, as Josie and he continue their trip to France and Spain.

A MEDITATION GONE AWRY

HARMONIC UNIVERSE ONE. Twenty-First Century. Planet Earth.

After their trip to Europe, Josie has to go visit her parents in Brazil, and Elliott finds himself alone in their apartment in California. He remembers Rita, the extraterrestrial shaman, and when he calls her, they set up an appointment for a meditation together.

The next day, Rita arrives at his place, and after a bit of chitchat they decide to go on a shamanic journey, mainly—according to Rita—to replace Elliott's lungs and upgrade his system for a full access to twelve-stranded DNA. Elliott is not fully on board with this mumbo jumbo, but he wants to go on a journey together with her. As such, he lies back in the crème suede sofa, while Rita relaxes in the red-clothed armchair. They close their eyes, and after a few words and incantations from Rita, he notices himself going into a trance state, which feels different from what he has experienced before. It is as if the front half of his body is in one plane of existence and the back side of his body is in the normal plane of existence. He is aware of his own presence in his dwelling, and at the same time, he is aware that the front side of his body is in a room with four individuals. And they are talking to him and about him.

"Elliott, we are going to upgrade your systems. Just relax. You are in capable hands."

"Rita, there are four guys here, and they seem to be working on me, and I currently feel more like a car going into maintenance than on a shamanic journey," whispers Elliott.

"I know," replies Rita. "You need this upgrade. There are too many hurdles for you to overcome to achieve why you have volunteered to be here. This is an accelerated growth for you."

To Elliott, it really feels like he is at a machine shop and he is the machine getting a service make over. There is not much further communication with his technicians, but he can hear a few things left and right, and he definitely feels things changing in his body.

"How do we replace the lung?" Technician One says.

"Through the mouth. Elliott, please open your mouth."

And Elliott complies by opening his mouth. He feels a liquid-like substance going in, extraction of what feels to be his lungs, and then the insertion of a liquid-like balloon substance that grows in his chest area.

"Hey check this out. Did you see that?" exclaims Technician Two.

Elliott feels light flashes in his chest cavity, and it seems like that light has its own mind and it wants to hide from the technicians. It quickly moves away to a very far distance; almost like it disappears into space.

"Where did that go? Do you know what it is?" asks Technician Two.

"No, but that was not supposed to be there. Make a note of it in the logs," answers Technician Three.

While this is going on, Rita tells Elliott that she has to stop her part of the meditation because of another engagement, and she leaves the apartment.

Overall, it is a very enjoyable, even though confusing, experience, and Elliott continues to bask in a blissful state until suddenly he feels a snap, like when a cable is cut. Suddenly his reality starts to shift, the awareness of his body in his apartment fades away, and he sees many movies streaming in and out. He becomes aware of a lot more realities, including one with a series of people that he recognizes as his friends. And when they become aware of his awareness of them, he hears them say in unison, "F——K," and they try to hide. Meantime, the realities passing by and through him become many more, thousands more, and it is very disorienting until he feels a hand grabbing him and three wonderful beings stand in front of him.

"Elliott, what have you done?"

Somehow, he clearly knows these beings are guardian angels, and he feels very familiar with them.

"I am meditating with an extraterrestrial. Why? Did something go wrong?" asks Elliott.

"We are checking into that. Well, you are not going to like what we are about to tell you, but you died."

"I did?" gasps Elliott. "But I am still alive. Look, we are talking with one another."

"Well, in that case, try to go back to your body," says one of the guardian angels.

Elliott focuses on linking back to his body. He has done this many times over in his journeys, and usually, it only takes a few moments to feel his body and slowly wake up from meditative journeys. This time, however, he cannot even locate his body, much less make a connection to go back into it.

"I can't go back to my body. Does that mean I really died?" asks Elliott.

"Well, you never really die, but let's just say that you are in transition because your experiential physical body was killed. We are your guardian angels. Let us show you what happened." And the guardian angel draws a circle with his hand which turns into a window. When Elliott looks through the window, he is looking from the ceiling down, and he can see his body in the crème suede sofa with a huge hole in his chest and blood splattered all around.

"Oh my! That does not look good," Elliott responds, shocked. It is quite overwhelming to see one's own body covered in blood and with a big gaping hole in the chest.

"What happened?"

"You were shot in the chest by an extraterrestrial from the Geeray collective. She teleported into your living room as soon as Rita left and fired a ray gun at your chest. For the record, this is a huge violation of many laws and this will have major repercussions for the perpetrators, including your controllers."

"What are controllers?"

"You will find that out shortly. In the meantime, we have to take you to a very special committee and you have a big decision to make. Do you want your life to continue or not?"

"I think so, yes," says Elliott.

"Well, you better be sure about it. You have been complaining quite a few times how hard it is to live down there, and some beings here are not convinced that you really want that life back. You are going in front of a committee, and if you really want to live out this life, you will have to convince them that your life back is what you want."

As the guardian angel finishes that sentence, a large white building appears in front of them, and Elliott find himself at the bottom of the white marble stairs. He is escorted up the stairs, and one of the three guardian angels holds open the door.

"We cannot follow you inside. Good luck, Elliott."

Elliott enters the large white building. It is enormous and magnificent. He walks toward the end of the building where three beings are seated behind a white marble table. He recognizes them as Vishnu, Shiva, and Brahma—the three supreme Gods that are revered in Hinduism.

Shiva calmly says, "State your business."

"Uhm . . ." Elliott lingers as he is trying to find his words. "I'm here to request the continuation of my life."

"Very well," says Vishnu. "Did you not state in previous experiences in your human life experience that you wanted it to end? That it was too hard? And that life should be enjoyable?"

"I don't remember the specific dates, but that is true yes. I probably have made those statements in my life."

"You made them more than once, and you even prayed for your life to end. So think carefully about what you are requesting. You could easily move on to your next experience, which would be more enjoyable than the current one."

"I know, and to be clear, I made those statements and prayers likely under emotional duress. I just feel like there is something that I still need to do there."

"Really? And what would that be?" says Brahma.

"I'm not sure. But I feel it in my gut. I think I am down there to help many."

"That is true, yes. But consider that your efforts may not be appreciated by many around and above you. And they might make it even more difficult to live where you came from. Would you want to take the chance to find that out and experience that much more pain and suffering?"

“I would take a chance on that. I do believe in love and in Supreme Love. I have only just gotten to remember the amazingness of All-That-Is, and I like these interactions.”

Shiva stresses his final words. “Do you stand by your decision to continue your prematurely interrupted human life experience? Yes? or No?”

“Yes.”

A nod follows by Vishnu, Brahma, and Shiva, and Shiva grabs a hammer. “Very well, then. You will continue your human life experience. Good luck and many blessings to you, Wise One.” And as Shiva strikes the marble table with the hammer a third time, Elliott wakes up in the crème suede sofa. Reflexively he grabs his chest; no blood or gaping holes are present.

“Oh my God, I’m back. And I’m fine. I’m really fine. Wow. You guys are good. Thank you!” spouts Elliott.

Many questions still remain in Elliott’s mind.

Who am I?

Why am I here?

How do I give meaning to my life, now that I have been resurrected?

These questions will be answered to him in the most painful and elating way, when he starts the second part of his journey, which will be revealed in The Chronicles of All-Time—Betrayal.

POEM TO SOURCE

A patient teacher, with passion and compassion,
A strong force with the wisdom to apply gently and Gentile,
See beauty everywhere, nowhere, now here.
No one undeserving, forever appreciating,
Longs to be known, to be rediscovered,
To be felt, to be admired, to be loved and cherished.
And yet never pulling or pushing, a gentle shepherd,
Awe and all-deserving, in constant motion,
A shower of colors, shapes, patterns, waves,
All in tune, in balance, at peace, perfect every moment,
And the next, and yet misunderstood.
A teacher doesn't punish, but alleviates ignorance.
You see, 'cause action creates reaction.
Be, do, have, and love, enjoy, be grateful,
Appreciate, be, and let be, it's that simple.
Yes, there is the Male and the Female,
The North and the South,
The rhythm of our lives abiding in time, in energy,
Good, good vibrations, like attracts like,
And like a bicycle, one paddle goes up and the other goes down.
Know who you are, where you are and with whom.

Be kind, be gentle, and love one another like your Self.
Miracles happen, savor them.
Honest work bears fruit; savor the journey.
Patience begets patience.
In the end We All are One, and the One is All,
To be savored, yearned for, and never fully understood until The End Beginning.
With Love, for Love, Love, Love.

Everything is connected.
As you do,
You will live.

Elliott learns about the true nature of his existence:
To bring peace across many dimensions,

To teach in the abstract and in the relative,

That we are one living being.

But first, can he overcome the deepest of betrayals and deceptions, and what does this mean to the rest of the Universe?

Find out in

The Chronicles of All-Time: Betrayal

Turn the page for a sneak preview

MEETING THE MAKER

HARMONIC UNIVERSE ONE. Twenty-First Century. Planet Earth.

Elliott is shaken up after dying a rather easy death. It is the meeting with the triumvirate committee that throws him off a bit. In the meeting, he had to ask for his human life experience to continue, rather than moving on to the next. And the coming back to this earthly plane is hard for him. It is like before he was swimming in a pristine crystal-clear tropical lagoon with the most exquisite sounds and colors, and as he came back to so-called Earth, he dived in a pit of putrid mud or sticky tar. He wonders why he chose to come back to this earthly existence. The amazing awesome-ness and elation and ecstasy that he experienced and remembers from the other side make it a lot harder to get used to everyday reality. To make matters even worse, he is starting to realize that his so-called normal life is merely an illusion, and the other side seems a lot more real, and definitely more enjoyable. For sure, he has a lot more friends and loved ones on the other-worldly planes. As such, it takes him a few days to go back to his daily routine of meditation. One afternoon, he is set on finding his path in life and the reason why he has come to this plane of existence, again. He lies down in bed and starts his meditation. Nothing much happens, and he is thinking maybe he lost his touch after taking a break. Just like having to start with less weights when one takes a break from going to the gym. He decides to wait a few minutes, and after a while, he feels energy scanning his body—not unpleasant though.

Meantime, close to planet Wakala, General H'Roc and his team are in the midst of hacking into the artificial reality where the ARC, also known as Elliott, resides.

"Captain, we have contact with the ARC. It is in meditative state, and the upload should start momentarily."

"Great work, ensign, transfer the ARC to our artificial reality and let me know when the download is completed."

"Yes, Captain."

Meantime, Elliott is experiencing moving through what he would call energy matrix wormholes, and he is quite excited at the new landscape that he is experiencing. Little does he know that he is being uploaded into a reality that will look exactly the same as the one where he used to reside, except that this time, he will not be treated favorably, but rather deceptively, and definitely not with his best interest at heart. His friends and family may look the same, but he will soon find out that they have been reduced to mere programs at the behest of the new controllers, General H'Roc and his team.

"Captain, we have a full download of the ARC and its environment, including the core matrices and probability algorithms for the characters that surround his reality experience."

"Excellent! First get us out of Intergalactic Federation space. Set a course for the Racoseta home world. Then, let's go play with the ARC and make sure that it complies with our desires. Let's make it our best friend so it trusts us and wants to do anything just to make us happy. S'Naf, you are our strategic officer. Can you create a program character that can serve as his Maker, which will be introduced by me?"

"Yes, General," says S'Naf. "That should not be problem. Just give me a few minutes."

Sergeant S'Naf busily works on a few basic algorithms and visual displays that he can choose from Elliott's memory and cultural background, and soon the character of Elliott's Maker is ready for use.

"The Maker character is ready, sir."

"Great, bring the probe online to go deep into the ARC's matrix to find where Commander Jane's consciousness has been linked and for uploading key tactical information about the Intergalactic Federation that she can provide us with. In doing so, we need to have full cooperation from the ARC drone, and I know exactly how to do that. Computer, activate three-dimensional display for the ARC's surroundings after last upload and activate microphone."

Computer voice: "Three-dimensional display activated. Microphone active."

In Elliott's bedroom, he suddenly hears a voice whispering, "Elliott, wake up. Open your eyes."

Elliott slowly opens his eyes, and in front of him he sees a pillar of white mist that is surging in a vertical flow. The mist stops flowing, and a large male figure with white hair appears from the mist.

General H'Roc regulates the flow of oxytocin in Elliott's brain, and a huge surge of this bonding hormone floods his brain. This hormone is usually only released in such quantities when a baby is born to induce bonding between the mother and the baby.

"I am your Maker."

Under influence of the hormone, Elliott experiences a huge level of elation, and he looks at the grand father figure with awe.

He utters, "Father!?"

"Yes, Elliott, I am your Father. I am your Maker. We do not have much time, young one. You are my one and only son. Do you understand that?"

"You mean, like Jesus?" asks Elliott.

"Much more than Jesus, Elliott. There is much to tell you, but right now, I need to ask you. Do you love me?"

"Yes! Yes, I love you very much."

"I want to establish a strong bond with you, my son. A marriage or a union as some call it. Would you please say yes to that?"

"A union?" blurts Elliott, and he is trying to think about it, but the oxytocin in his brain pushes him toward bonding. The outcome is inevitable.

"Yes, I would love that. How do we do that?"

"I only need your permission, dearly beloved. Please lie down, and I will come into you. This will take a while, but rest assured, I will take care of you. Do not be afraid. Trust love."

"OK, let me lie down on the bed." And Elliott closes his eyes.

General H'Roc disengages the microphone and yells, "Activate the probe and send it into the ARC now."

Instead of gentle energy enveloping Elliott, he senses a large energy substance enter him and move down deep within him. He smiles, assuming that he is undergoing a union with his Maker, rather than suspecting that he is being played as a pawn in an intergalactic war. After almost an hour of many feelings in his body and beyond, he feels the energy leaving his body, and he feels drained and tired. Elliott falls asleep.

"Captain, we have retrieved the probe, and we have scanned for access codes from Commander Darkon's consciousness. There is no trace of Commander Jane Darkon's within the ARC. We detected huge energy fields, but these may be random fluctuations in subspace particles that we picked up and definitely not linked to the Intergalactic Federation. Only random white noise, sir."

"That is impossible. Can you do a second scan?"

"Yes, sir, and we are already recalibrating the ARC and scanning every bit of its existence, but so far, there is not a sign of a second layer of recognizable consciousness."

"How long does it take to do another scan?"

"A few seconds, sir."

"Do it, now!"

"Affirmative," responds S'Naf, and after a few seconds, he says, "All findings are negative, sir."

"Set up a secure subspace channel with Dr. Brobol. I want to have a chat with him."

"Dr. Brobol is currently unavailable, sir. Would you like to leave a message?"

"No, let's try again later. Let the ARC matrix run its course. I'll decide later what to do with it."

"ARC matrix initialized and set on auto-configuration, Captain."

None of the crew pays any attention to what is happening in the artificial reality of the ARC. Its reality is fabricated on a so-called planet Earth, where he lives with many other artificial intelligent matrices within the core matrix of a time-based system in the twenty-first century. They call themselves humans, but that is far off from the original design of the first humans.

PRIME CREATOR EXPLAINS WHAT IS REALLY GOING ON

HARMONIC UNIVERSE ONE. Twenty-First Century. Planet Earth.

Elliott wakes up at two o'clock in the morning, knowing he is in the presence of Creator.

"*Come, young one, get out of bed. It is time to write.*"

"*Now? Really?*"

"*Yes. Now.*"

"*You mean at this very instant now?*" Elliott says again.

And Creator replies softly, "*Yes.*"

Elliott lingers rejuvenated, throws the purple bed sheets to the side, and runs upstairs to get his notepad and a pen.

"*What do you want me to write about?*"

"*Write about your journey and, now that you have learned discernment, add your thoughtful analysis to the events that led you where you are now. First, introduce yourself the way you were before I pulled you out of your body into Heaven.*"

Elliott asks just for the sake of relieving doubt. "*Are you really Creator?*"

"*I am that, I am that I am. You are bit shy, so allow Me to do the talking?*"

"*Yes, please.*"

"*First, at your current time/space coordinates, the embodiment that carries what you are is not directly created by Myself, even though, from an absolute perspective, one can conceive that I am the Creator of everything, so my former statement of Me not being your Creator is up for debate. It depends on perspective. You were born in a galaxy far, far away. Before your physical manifestation, your Soul was crafted by Myself. Yes, there are highly evolved beings whose purpose is to create Souls, but You were made by Me, from Me, through Me and carefully tutored by Me. You did not come here to learn, but to teach and to transform. The arrival of a so-called 'Chosen One' is expected in many worlds throughout worlds and is sought after by many individuals. Some have Your best interest at heart, some mean to exploit You, and some seek to destroy You. As such, it is vital that you are protected at all times before you become aware of Who you truly are and that your identity is kept secret at all times, even from yourself. As such, whole layers of holographic memory inserts with light, thought, feeling and sound encoded locks are kept in place, and they are to be released one after the other by random events that have been predetermined, so that carefully, event after event, a new personality arises that reflects clearer and better who you truly are. You writing this under My Guidance is one of the final steps. You have entered 'physicality' when your Soul merged to a physical body. This process of bonding a Soul to a human vehicle is very delicate and starts about one to three months after conception, and is completed usually by the middle of the third trimester. Because of the Essence that you carry, your human mother could not complete her pregnancy to full term. Her body could not handle the higher frequencies that you were pulling in, and, as such, you were released from the womb prematurely, and she mentioned many times later in your development that you were born too early.*

"The birth of a Soul is overseen by the angelic realm, and so was yours. Under the guise of an 'indigo/crystal child,' we assigned Archangel Metatron and Archangel Michael along with two other guardian angels (Uriel and Gabriel) to watch over you from the minute you were born. As you correctly stated earlier, every Soul that is birthed gets the same attention as every other Soul, because you are All equal. As I explained to you earlier, there is a difference between someone's Spirit and their Soul. The Soul is your God-Self, infinite, all-knowing, all-loving. Your Spirit is the amount of energy/consciousness that can be anchored in your energy bodies that are linked to your physical body made manifest. As such, the Spirit is at any given time finite, and, as long as the connection with God or the Soul is maintained, its energy can be replenished indefinitely during e.g. sleep, meditation, altered states of consciousness.

"You were brought up in a normal home with two loving parents who tried to give you all that you need. Your biological parents were

unaware—at a human consciousness level—about your true nature as it was meant that you were raised as normal as possible without the reverie that would otherwise ensue. Through you father you were taught to divert your attention away from the Catholic Church and to hold logic as your primary way of dealing with information. The idea of God was buried between well-meant intentions and the four pillars of your dad's moral code:

> *Do unto others what you want others to do unto you.*
> *Work hard and reap the rewards.*
> *Never compare yourself to anyone else (neither better, nor worse).*
> *Make your own self and don't be owned by allegiances or debts or favors to anyone else.*

"Some of these four pillars are causing your conflict right now. While you fully agree with the first and the third pillar, your Soul knows that if you let Source be your guide, then all that you need—including money—is supplied. Yes, money can grow on trees or can be added to your checking account in the blink of an eye in a truly free Universe, but you are not living in a truly free Universe right now. Mind you that sometimes you are in a constrained reality where the Maker of that Universe has set forth rules that need to be obeyed in order to manifest your desires, such as productivity, integrity, cleanliness, and order. In this case, it is much harder to manifest from your thoughts only. The fourth pillar is where you agree not to be bound by anyone, and yet you know that unconditional surrender to the Divine will bring exaltation in a truly free Universe. Mind you that surrendering all to the Divine can be tricky business in a constrained reality—for brave Souls only.

"What you do not know about that famous night in May when you met Me is that your drink was spiked with a drug by one of your best friends. It was meant to create the illusory meeting between God and yourself, and that interaction was carefully orchestrated by beings from another dimension. And guess who gave them that idea? Me. And you really did talk to Me through My intervention. Little did they know that drugging you was part of the Divine Plan to wake you up for real. God works in mysterious ways.

"Much earlier in your life, you became a target when you signed up for a blood screen in Chicago in 2005. You see, in some cultures it is prophesized

that 'a happy person of human descent would radiate so much light and end the enslavement of many.' More on that later.

"You became a target when the blood screen highlighted that you are a carrier of the genetic background that is able to house and transmit ultrahigh frequencies (UHF), and as such, you can remember and tell the long-lost knowledge that was buried with the Fall of Atlantis. This Sacred Knowledge has been kept by many untold saints and heroes before your arrival, as well as by 'The People Within,' who live in Agartha and other Inner Earth locations. You became a target for infiltration and systematic invasion to make sure that your true nature was subdued, never to be awakened, or if so, you would be guided on a wild goose chase that would lead to nothing but disappointment, sadness, resentment, and eventually, enslavement leading to your ultimate scheduled demise. Many of your friends have their own agenda, and many games are played at many levels. First, there is the level of those who truly think this is just a game being played. These friends think you are overreacting to circumstances, and some will decide not to play with you anymore. What they do not know is that under their nose, your Spirit is being primed for a lifetime enslavement, which you will be able to live in excruciating detail.

"Oh, Elliott, there is much to teach you, and you may not be able to absorb all of this, but it serves you to delve into it at a later stage. Please get comfortable with this matter and then I will explain you more what is going on. Time matters when it matters. Make haste peacefully. Much love to you, my dear little one."

Edwards Brothers Malloy
Oxnard, CA USA
December 10, 2014